VAMPIRE
HUNTER SOCIETY
The Dark Soul

PURGING EVIL, ONE
VAMPIRE AT A TIME

Leia Stone

I SAT up with a scream on my lips and my eyelids snapped open. I was in a room I didn't recognize, but the two figures hunched over my bed were terribly familiar.

The first thing I noticed was my throat felt like it was made of sandpaper and my head burned like it had been sliced open.

Luka and Liv stared at me in shock, eyes red-rimmed like they'd both been crying. Memories flooded my mind then: Morgana shooting and killing me, my body floating into the beautiful peaceful light. Luka … biting me, feeding me his blood.

Changing me?

I clawed at my throat, feeling like I might die all over again. Then Luka snapped into action. Walking over to a refrigerator, he pulled out two bottles of dark crimson fluid.

"This will be easier to—" His words barely registered as I flew across the room and snatched the bottles from his hand. Ripping off the lid, I pressed the rim of the bottle to my lips and tipped it backward.

The second the thick cold fluid hit my tongue, an explosion of flavor burst across my mouth. A deep moan ripped from my throat as I gulped it down. It was like chocolate and strawberries and ... *sex.* Or at least what I imagined sex would be. My brain wasn't really thinking. All I needed in this entire world was for this overwhelming thirst to be quenched.

"Okay this is *awkward.*" Liv's voice brought me back to the present and Luka chuckled.

"The first drink is the best. It will dull over time but not completely," he responded.

Then I noticed it: the lack of heartbeat, no longer needing to breathe, the thick crimson fluid having the slightest metallic iron taste.

I looked at the empty bottle in my hand and my fingers went up to probe my teeth. "I'm a bloodsucker," I mumbled against my fingers.

Two sharp points pressed against my fingertips and I gasped, dropping the empty container to the ground and lifting my clean shirt to stare at my abdomen. No holes. No scars to even show where the bullets had entered my body.

"I mean you were good looking before... but dayuuuuuum," Liv declared.

I blinked rapidly at my best friend. It had worked. Luka had turned me into a vampire.

"I need a mirror." I scrambled out of the room and into the adjoining bathroom.

"Take it easy! You're still changing, you don't know your—" Luka's voice was stopped by me flipping the light switch up so fast and hard that it snapped off, the little plastic nub falling to the floor.

"...strength," he finished.

With the light illuminating my face, I looked up into the mirror and froze.

"God help me," I breathed.

I was a vampire: paper white skin, red-tinged lips, pointed canines, eerie stillness, but it was the eyes that freaked me out. My eyes were no longer human. Yellow rings stared back at me.

"You *asked* me to, remember? You gave me permission," Luka hedged, looking at me frightened, like I might attack him or something.

I nodded, my head still reeling. I should cry, I should pray, I should have some sort of reaction, but all I could think about in that moment was how thirsty I was. "Need more," I growled, and Luka nodded to my hand.

Oh. I was still holding one of the bottles. I popped the lid and tipped it back, before looking at Luka expectantly.

"Right." He rushed out and returned with two fresh bottles.

I took them inside the bathroom and shut the door on Luka, leaning back against it and sliding down to the floor as I chugged blood from some unwitting donor.

What was my mom going to say? Maple? What about freaking Ruby, who was due here today? This was a mess.

My stomach burned with hunger, and dizziness washed over me.

"More!" I yelled, and two seconds later there was a knock.

I opened the door a few inches and Luka pushed two more bottles through.

I slammed the door, chugging the bottles, feeling disgusted with myself.

This was too much blood. Six bottles? Or eight? I'd lost count. Luka never fed like this. What was wrong with me?

There was a knock and I peeled the door open a crack.

Luka cleared his throat. "You might need a few more. The first feeding is what really cements the change." He looked sad, or maybe scared. I knew I should reassure him that I wasn't mad at him, but I couldn't right now. Because I *was* mad. I was mad at Morgana for doing this to me, mad that Liv convinced me to change, mad at everyone involved. I missed the light, I missed the free weightless feeling of death. Reaching out, I grabbed two more bottles and shut the door again. This time, when I brought it to my lips, the taste of the iron was heavier and the chocolate and strawberries less.

I was getting used to it.

Sick.

Gross.

Frick!

I wanted to throw up, go back, just die by the side of the road.

"Aspen." Luka's tender voice reached through the door and wrapped around my heart.

Tears filled my eyes as the severity of the situation pressed in on me.

I wasn't human…

God forgive me, I pled as a sob formed in my throat.

I scooched forward and opened the door wide, and then Luka stepped inside, kneeling before me.

"I'm sorry."

Those two words made the walls come down and I burst into hysterical sobs as he took me in his arms. My chest shook; grief tore through me as I mourned my human body. My soul. My old life. Normalcy. I cried over it all and Luka just held me. At one point, I heard the front door open and close a few times, but I just continued to cry. Liv must have left, but I couldn't stop. The grief, the shock, the suddenness of it all just poured out of me.

Luka stroked my cheek. "Emotions are heightened and erratic in the first few days and weeks. This is normal."

Nothing about being a bloodsucker was normal. *I just drank ten bottles of blood!* So far from freaking normal. But I said nothing. My sobs turned to whimpers, which eventually quieted, and I wiped my eyes.

Reaching out, I touched my neck with two fingers. "I don't have a pulse."

Luka nodded. "It will take getting used to. You won't poop or pee anymore either."

"What!" I screamed, and reeled back.

Luka gave me a slow grin. "The blood is fully absorbed and you just don't."

What the crap? Out of all the things that had happened in the last day, that had shocked me the most.

There was a knock at the bathroom door and then Liv's voice came from the other side. "You okay, Aspen?"

My heart pinched. She was probably worried about me and I'd pushed her away to have a nervous breakdown. Luka released me and I stood waaay faster than normal and the bathroom spun.

"Slow down, cowboy. It takes getting used to," Luka warned.

Right.

I tried to act like a turtle would and opened the door slowly, looking up at my bestie. There were unshed tears in her eyes and she chewed her lip.

"I just didn't want to lose you. It was selfish but—"

I crashed into her and squeezed, but not too hard, as she hugged me back. "You are really fast. That freaked me out," she admitted.

I grinned, pulling away. "I don't blame either of you," I told them, and they both looked relieved.

"I blame that bitch Morgana, and now that I'm her equal I'm going to rip her head off and shove it up her ass!" I growled.

Luka's eyebrows shot up. "Easy there, killer. Morgana fled, but I've got the entire realm looking for her. She killed the fiancée of the vampire king. It's a crime punishable by death."

"Except I'm not dead! They will probably let her go with a slap on the wrist," I growled.

Luka's lips pursed. "Don't worry about Morgana. We have bigger things to deal with."

"Like what?" I scoffed. "I'm a vampire now. The council will allow us to get married and you can remain king."

He nodded, sharing a look with Liv. "Yes. That's all fine."

I pinned my man with a glare. "What aren't you telling me?"

Both he and Liv took a step backward into the hallway. "Just stay calm, okay. The first few days—"

"Stop telling me about the first this and that. What's wrong?" I bellowed, clenching my fists.

Luka frowned, looking to Liv.

"Olivia Rose, start talking or so help me God…" I looked at my best friend and she nodded.

"House of Thorns showed up while you were … healing," she said.

Oh. Ruby was already here! It would be a shock for her to see me like this, but I wanted to get a head start on our plan to save the other breeders. "Okay, I'll shower and explain everything to her. She'll understand."

It's not like I asked to become a bloodsucker. I was dying—she'd see reason in what had to be done. *Hopefully.*

Liv shook her head. "No, Aspen. They showed up *without* Ruby. She was taken." Her gaze flicked again to Luka. "We think by Maz."

Pure unbridled rage worked its way up my body. My hands started to shake. I needed to go after her. Ruby was in trouble because I'd told her to come and bring her whole team here. Maz must have found out. The anger was too much. It bubbled inside of me like hot lava and I was going to explode. I was a blur of motion as I streaked across the room and grabbed the dresser leaning against the wall.

"Aspen!" Liv cried out.

"Just stay back," Luka warned, pulling Liv behind him.

I picked up the dresser high into the air and

threw it on the ground, splintering it into a hundred pieces.

"That evil hag," I roared, punching my fist into the wall. There was a sharp pain for a moment as it collided with brick, but then it was gone. The stone burst outward, and I retracted my hand, which had now blown a hole the size of a pumpkin into the wall. I looked out at the garden and felt remorse for destroying the wall, but my anger at Maz was too hard to control. I needed a physical outlet or I was going to kill someone.

"Stop her, she'll hurt herself," Liv pleaded with Luka behind me.

"She could hurt *me* right now," he replied to her. "Besides, I've always wanted a garden view in this room."

I wanted to laugh, I wanted to tell Liv I was totally fine, but I was so damn mad I couldn't think straight.

Maz kidnapped Ruby and it was all my fault. I wanted to *kill* someone.

"My love." Luka approached me with his hands out, like you would come at a lion. "Running helps. Would you like to go for a run with me?"

My chest heaved. "I want to break shit and kill someone!" I growled.

Liv backed up to the wall, and shame rushed through me for scaring her. These emotions weren't me, I knew that. It was the change or whatever, but it felt so real.

Luka motioned to the front door. "Okay, run instead?"

"Fine!" I growled, unable to control the whirlwind of hatred I was dealing with.

One second I charged forward and opened the door, and the next I was on the garden lawn breathing in the fresh air.

"I may not *need* to breathe but I'm still going to do it!" I snarled at Luka.

He smirked. "Whatever makes you happy."

Bastard was too nice for me right now.

He took off then, like a streak of lightning. He tore from the garden and through the castle grounds, and all of my rage reached fever pitch. I ran after him, pumping my legs and arms so fast I thought I might fall over.

I hated change. I didn't want to be a vampire. I didn't want to be this fast. I was annoyed, and pissed at everything. But as I ran, this discordant energy burned through me and gave way to a sliver of my normal self. I didn't care where we were going, I just followed Luka. Farmlands, cars, a city, we passed so much, and I relished the feeling of the wind in my hair and the lightness of my feet. I could tell Luka was really exerting himself to lead the run. He looked a bit worn out by the time we stopped in front of a thick stretch of woods.

"It's gone," I said, feeling for that blind rage and finding it minimal. I was relieved.

Luka nodded. "I tore a car in half after Morgana changed me against my will."

My upper lip curled. "Morgana," I growled.

"But let's not talk about that!" Luka interjected, wrapping an arm around me and pulling me toward the sound of running water.

I trudged along the wooded path with Luka until we reached a small creek. I felt my frayed nerves soothe a bit. Luka sat on a large smooth stone at the water's edge and I plopped down next to him.

We sat there in silence, Luka stealing glances my way every few minutes.

"What?" I pressed him.

He let out a shaky breath. "I thought I'd lost you. I didn't know if it would work."

My heart squeezed. This whole time I'd been wrestling with becoming a vampire and Luka had thought I was going to die. I nodded, remembering the light, the amazing feeling of being weightless and being encompassed by so much love. "You didn't tell me how beautiful it was to die."

A half smile pulled at his lips. "It's like that for all of us. For a few seconds there's the light and the feeling of complete peace."

I nodded. "I didn't want to leave."

"I didn't either," he agreed. "Can you ever forgive me?"

His face pulled taut with grief, and I realized I'd been so torn up over my situation I hadn't assured him enough about us.

"Well, I have to now! We're about to be married for quite literally *forever*." I grinned.

The smile that graced Luka's face then was a full-on beam. "So you're still marrying me?"

My heart fell into my stomach over the fact that he thought any of my feelings on that might have changed.

"Luka, I love you." I leaned forward and placed a hand on his chest. He turned and my lips brushed his. Chills raced down my spine at the intensity of the feeling and I shivered.

"Everything will be heightened. Smell, taste, touch, emotions, strength, speed, you have to go easy with everything."

I nodded, looking out at the creek. The trickling

water caused a loud and uncomfortable rushing sound in my eardrums if I focused on it too long. I was about to ask Luka something, when a thought struck me.

"Oh my gosh, you haven't fed from me! Is our bond broken? Can you sense my feelings?"

'I can,' Luka said in my mind and I jumped.

"Oh crap, it didn't work. Luka!" I let out a sob. How long since he'd eaten? My blood was dead now and wouldn't feed him, I—

He grinned. "Calm down. I drank from Liv. It worked."

I frowned, jealously spiking through me. "You drank from my best friend!"

Luka paled. "It was an emergency situation, until I could get the bottled blood."

Bastard. These emotions were too intense. I didn't feel like myself. "From now on, you only drink from wrinkly old ladies or bottles!" I snarled.

He chuckled. "Deal."

"I'm sorry I'm being crazy. I don't feel like myself…" I admitted.

He nodded. "The hormones, cell repair, it's all doing its thing. You will feel better in a few weeks, I promise."

'How can I still hear you in my head?' I asked.

"Well, besides the fact that I'm your sire and you my fledgling, I'm your king. I have a mental connection to all of my vampires, though not as strong."

Whoa. Like an alpha werewolf. That was kinda cool.

I snuggled into his side and he wrapped his arm around me.

"Luka?"

"Yes, my love?"

"I'm going to wake up tomorrow and still want to kill Maz and Morgana. I hope you know that."

His body stiffened next to me, but he wisely said nothing. I could rip the head off a bear right now and he knew it. Best to keep his mouth shut.

"HOLY HOTNESS!" Demi squealed as Sage's mouth hit the floor.

Luka and I had gotten back from our run about an hour ago and I'd made Liv tell my mom, Maple, Demi, and Sage what had happened because I was too chicken. I still hadn't seen my mom and Maple, but Sage and Demi insisted on checking in on me. We were in Luka's quarters in the castle, which encompassed two large master bedrooms, a sitting room, a kitchen, and an indoor hot tub gazebo. I sat on the couch of the sitting room. Demi and Sage were frozen in the doorway.

"You're like a porcelain doll!" Sage breathed, stepping closer.

I chuckled. "Hey."

Demi's face fell as she approached me. "I'm so

sorry. I know you didn't want this, but I'm so glad you're still with us."

She crossed the room quickly and sat next to me, pulling me into a hug. I wrapped my arms around her, hugging her back and taking care to not squeeze, but instead lightly rested my arms on her back. I knew she was a werewolf, but I didn't want to break the ribs of the alpha.

"Thanks. It's been emotional," I admitted.

Demi nodded. "And which bitch do we need to kill for doing this to you?"

Luka coughed from his place by the window. "We will table any retaliation plans until Aspen is feeling herself again."

Sage rolled her eyes at him. "You're no fun."

"Was it Morgana?" Demi asked in a low whisper.

"I'm a vampire, I can hear you," Luka muttered.

"Yep. And she's mine!" I growled, and slammed my fist into the coffee table, which splintered and broke in half.

Oops.

Demi looked unfazed by my rage, nodding. "We will help you find her when the time comes."

"In the meantime..." Luka pushed off his place at the wall near the window. "I need to talk to you and Sawyer. We've got a fey problem."

Demi nodded. "I heard. The Ithaki lands touch mine, Luka."

"Heard what?" I asked.

Luka rubbed the back of his neck. "I didn't want to bother you with it."

"Speak," I snapped.

Sage and Demi both grinned.

"Two Ithaki women were taken. We think the fey might be trying to start a new breeder camp and we want to shut it down before—"

"How dare they!" I snarled, squeezing my thigh so hard I thought I might snap my own femur.

"Right. Well, we need to decide if we are going to go after the wo—"

"If you want to marry me in two days, you will go after the women!" I grumbled.

Sage's eyebrows shot up and Luka gave a peal of nervous laughter. "The first few days and weeks of the change can be emotional."

I stood. "Call me emotional. One. More. Time..."

I couldn't control the anger, it just kept coming, and I hated it. I was so mad, *so* mad that I'd been ripped away from the beautiful light floating feeling, so mad Morgana forced Luka's hand. And that Maz took Ruby—and now more innocent women would be forced into a breeding situation. "Going for a run!

I need to be alone," I snapped, and took off out of the palace.

This wasn't me. I wasn't mean to people like this, people I loved. I wasn't uncontrollable with my emotions. My anger turned to sadness and a sob rattled my chest as I zoomed through the garden and out into the great open lands of Vampire City. So much drama had happened the past few weeks. I couldn't process it all.

I'd never eat another bacon cheeseburger.

I'd never get sick again.

I'd never go poop, for crying out loud! This wasn't normal.

Then it hit me, what was really making me so angry, so heartbroken. I hadn't fully grieved the fact that I'd never carry my own child. Cassara had carved out my womb and I hadn't processed that. Sure, a few eggs had been frozen, but it wasn't a guarantee. Another sob ripped from my throat and I fell to my knees in a field of lavender, my back heaving as the emotions that I'd tucked away as a human were torn to the surface like a hurricane that unearthed dead bodies and hidden secrets.

I may never hear the word mommy.

All I ever wanted was a family. Growing up an

orphan, I wanted to have a child and give her something I never had: a mom and dad.

Footsteps approached at my back and I swear I
was ready to rip Luka's head off for following me. I
hated him seeing me like this, like a crazy woman
who couldn't control herself. Stupid hormones.
Stupid changing vampire body.

I turned, ready to throat punch him, when Sage's
cinnamon colored wolf walked over to me with her
tail tucked between her legs.

My sob turned to a whimper, and she nuzzled up
to my chest like a dog would. Reaching out, I
wrapped my arms around her and exhaled all of my
rage and grief. I couldn't handle a human right now,
but a fluffy animal that didn't talk was just what I
needed, and Sage seemed to understand that. She lay
on my lap as I stroked her fur and let the emotions
swirl around me.

At one point, I laughed like a lunatic at how
crazy my life had become. Meeting Luka that night
at the club had been the turning point of my entire
life, and somehow it had led me to here: sitting in a
field of lavender with a werewolf on my lap while I
cried and lost my mind about being turned into a
vampire.

The sun started to set. I had a vague thought that

I should eat dinner, but then I remembered that I no longer ate and it just depressed me again.

"I'm ready to go back," I told Sage, getting one last pet in. She nodded her head and then stood, shaking her fur out. Then she looked up at me with her tongue lolled to the side and tail wagging like a dog.

I grinned. "Wanna race?"

Without warning, she took off through the field, back toward the castle. I burst from where I stood and ran after her. "Cheater!" I called, laughter bubbling up inside of me.

The past hour, I'd felt calm and more like myself. I was hoping it meant that this emotional roller-coaster ride was over. Sage was fast, but I was faster. I caught up to her easily and she growled in frustration, which caused me to grin. By the time we made it to the garden, the sun had almost fully set and the sky was bathed in oranges and golds.

Luka and Demi were sitting on the stone bench talking, and I slowed my pace, kicking up some grass as I came to an abrupt halt.

Luka looked over at me sleepily. Vampire sleep time was in the day, and he had probably stayed awake for me. Seeing him now, I felt the weight of sleep pull at my limbs. Thank God vampires still slept. I wasn't sure I could handle being awake 24/7 forever on top of having to drink blood.

"Tired?" he asked.

I nodded. "And feeling better."

Everyone looked relieved at that. No more crazy lady breaking furniture. "But I should probably go talk to House of Thorns, they are most likely freaking out—"

"Liv is on it. You can see them tomorrow, rest with me." He held out his hand and I nodded. Turning back to look down at Sage's wolf form, I bent to one knee and scratched her behind the ears. "Thank you, friend," I whispered. "I won't forget that."

She nuzzled my palm and Demi stepped over to me, wishing Luka a good night. When she opened her arms to me, I fell into them and gave her a hug. "Say the word and we hunt that Morgana bitch down," she growled softly in my ear.

"I can *hear* you," Luka added, and I grinned.

Pulling back from Demi, I met her gaze. "I'll let you know."

She gave me a curt nod, pulling her long braid over one shoulder, and I noticed her t-shirt today said *MILF.*

I chuckled.

I'd lucked out making these new friends, especially since it looked like I was going to be living here *forever*.

"Oh shit. Am I … gonna become the vampire queen?" My mouth popped open with the sudden realization, and Demi looked to Luka expectantly.

"Yes … I mean, if you want to," he hedged, probably scared I would pick up the stone bench and chuck it across the garden.

"I mean, I want to be your wife, so…" I threw my arms up in confusion. Former vampire hunter now *queen* of the vampires? I'm not sure how beloved I would be to my people.

He smiled. "Then you will be queen. Package deal."

"Glad to hear you will be staying king," Demi said as she and Sage started to walk out of the garden. "Sawyer and my plan for Morgana as queen was not pretty and involved a lot of explosives."

I chuckled.

"Night," Luka told her.

"Night," she said.

When they were gone, it was just us. Two people with no heartbeats who didn't poop.

"So no more bacon cheeseburgers?"

Luka chuckled. "I mean … you can, but it's not pretty when it tries to come out undigested."

Gross.

With a small grin, he reached out and scooped me into his arms, cradling me against his chest.

"I know it wasn't a choice you made with excitement, but now that we have forever together, I promise to give you the most amazing life, Aspen Rose."

Well, if that wasn't swoon worthy, I didn't know what was.

I'D SLEPT, which was weird, because I was a freaking vampire now! When I'd woken up next to Luka, I went to the bathroom and sat on the toilet like I always did, and when no pee came out I'd burst into tears for a second before laughing maniacally. Okay, maybe some of my crazy emotions were still processing. But not peeing anymore? It was just weird.

Now we sat across from each other holding our warm bottled breakfast. "Cheers!" I tapped my bottle of blood to Luka's and he chuckled. "You're surprisingly okay with this."

I shrugged. "I'm definitely going to be hiring a full-time shrink. Do we have those here?"

He shook his head. "But I can get you one from Spokane that knows about the supernatural world."

I waved him off, chugging the fourth bottle of blood and trying to wrap my head around my new life. "I'm ready to meet with House of Thorns. I gotta find Ruby and—"

Luka's eyebrows rose. "Babe, our wedding is supposed to be tomorrow."

Shit.

I'd forgotten the small, ill-planned affair.

"What's wrong?" Panic flooded his face. "You *do* still want to get married, right?"

I leapt across the room a little too quickly, and bumped into him.

Oops. "Sorry. Still figuring out the speed and strength thing."

He chuckled, but there was a look of fear on his face. Reaching out, I cupped his chin. "Luka, I am so totally marrying you. I just ... always thought my wedding would be, like, a big planned-out event with all my friends, and a four-tier cake, and custom dress, in a church ... but I know time is an issue and money might be tight—"

Luka reached out and placed a finger to my lips,

stopping my rambling midsentence. "Say no more, my love."

I frowned. "What do you mean?"

"Now that you are a vampire, the council will give me an extension. Money is *not* an issue. All of our people pay a crown tax, and I want to give you the wedding of your dreams."

Our people. Vampires were now *my people.*

Tears filled my eyes and I nodded, offhandedly wondering how I could cry but not pee. I guessed that was not a good question to ask right now.

Luka pressed his lips to mine and a slight moan escaped me. In all the drama of my change, and passing out last night because I was so tired, I hadn't really touched or kissed him. Now that I had, it was like an inferno had ignited inside of me. With more force than I intended, I threw him backward onto the love seat and straddled him. His head hit the pillow hard and he looked up at me with a grin. Leaning forward, I dragged my tongue across his bottom lip and he groaned.

"You kill me, woman."

My smile widened and I moved to his neck, peppering him with kisses along his collarbone. Reaching up, I pulled his shirt up to reveal his perfect, tan, tattooed abs.

Yum. Moving my head down, I trailed my tongue across his stomach, enjoying the frantic panting he was exhibiting.

I got to the first button of his jeans and popped it open.

"Aspen," he moaned.

I was about to unbutton the second one when a knock came at the door.

"GO AWAY!" Luka roared.

"It's Liv!" she yelled. "We got news on Ruby!"

I froze.

"Go away. She'll meet you in ten minutes!" Luka roared back, and I burst into laughter.

Pulling my head up, I met his golden yellow gaze. "I'm sorry, babe. I gotta help with Ruby. It was partly my fault Maz was tipped off to her."

Luka took in a deep breath and closed his eyes. When they opened, they were nearly glowing, and centered on mine. "I'm going to destroy you on our wedding night."

That fire was back inside of me and I leaned forward, pressing a kiss to his lips. "Promise?"

As I walked away, I enjoyed the growl that ripped from his throat.

THE TEMPORARY HOUSING Luka had put the House of Thorns in was way nicer than I expected. The floor of the barn was concrete, not dirt, and it was fully insulated, with running water and electricity. Rows and rows of triple, high bunk beds lined the space, with a little meeting area to the front of the room that had various chairs, beanbags, and couches. It was actually quite comfortable for their group of over sixty people.

I'd walked in with Liv and she'd told me that she'd warned everyone that I'd been changed into a vampire to save my life due to a freak accident, but still they stared. Fingers twitched as if looking for a weapon, and their eyes slitted in accusation.

I would fear me too. Liv and I of all people knew

what it was like to leave that life and find out it was all a lie.

"Aspen!" a familiar voice said.

I spun, mouth hanging open as Vasquez ran toward me.

I looked at Liv in shock. "You didn't tell me!"

She smiled. "He got here an hour ago with news of Ruby. Surprise."

I burst forward and we crashed together, old childhood friends. The air whooshed out of Vaz's lungs. "Ouch," he huffed and I realized my hold was too strong.

"Sorry. I'm new." I pulled back and took him in. He was fully suited up for hunting, stakes and all; his chin was scabbed over and bleeding.

"It's … going to take some getting used to," he said, eyes lingering on my lips, which I now wondered if they were tinged red from my "break-fast" with Luka.

Seeing Vaz made me think of Sterling and my heart pinched in sorrow.

"Vaz, I'm so sorry we brought you and Sterling into this." I looked down at his feet, unable to meet his eyes.

Reaching out, he tipped my chin up. "I'd rather

die knowing the truth than live a lie. Sterling was the same."

That made me feel a little bit better. "What news do you have of Ruby?"

Vaz sighed. "I was laying low at my cousin's, like Sterling told me to, when Ruby started to contact me. We talked every day until her calls stopped."

I frowned. They must have been sharing info on everything and trying to put the puzzle pieces together.

"So I came out to Spokane to check on her and saw that the House of Thorns had been burned to the ground. Everyone gone."

I gasped and Liv nodded. "She got everyone out but it's ruined," she said.

Holy crap. It had to be Maz.

Vaz ran a hand through his dark hair. "So I started thinking. If I wanted to find Ruby and I figured Maz had her, I just needed to find Maz."

I snort-laughed. "Please tell me you didn't try to break into House of Rose. You'd be a dead man."

It was the most secure building in the inland Northwest. He shook his head. "I'm not crazy. But I do know a lot about the woman that raised us. Especially when she brags about seeing her beloved blade maker on—"

"Tuesdays!" Liv and I yelled in unison.

Every Tuesday, Maz picked up the House of Rose weapons. Some were new and some were just old blades getting sharpened, but Maz liked to go herself. We all thought she had a bit of a crush on the blade maker.

"And!" I flapped my hands, urging him to go on.

He nodded. "She had Ruby with her, bound and gagged in the car."

I frowned. Why would she be bringing Ruby around with her? Why hadn't she killed her yet?

"Aspen, I think Ruby is the lure," Vaz told me. "She's setting a trap to pull you and Liv to her so that she can kill you and stop you from saving the other women in the breeder encampments."

"Well, good, then she is going to get her wish." I cracked my knuckles and grit my teeth.

Vaz shook his head. "No. Ruby wouldn't want that. She'd want you to lead her team and continue her work. Save the six other encampments we have data on."

"You and Liv can start planning that. I'll get Ruby and be back by tomorrow." Rage rose up inside of me. How dare Maz do this? How dare she be such a two-faced liar? "If she wants to lure me out, then she's going to get her wish. I'll rip her head from her shoulders with my bare hands!" I screamed.

Liv suddenly swam into view, placing her hands on my shoulders. "Okay, Rambo. Just breathe. We'll figure it all out, but you can't go storming off with no plan."

I realized then that I'd bent the metal chair back I'd been leaning on. People were staring. Damn new vampire hormones.

"Sorry," I muttered.

"You're not going anywhere without me." Luka's voice came from behind me and I turned. The whole room had fallen into a hushed silence as they stared at the king of the vampires.

"Fair enough," I told my hubby-to-be.

He approached Vasquez, who stiffened, and then Luka looked around the room. "How are the accommodations?"

"Fine. Thank you," Vaz answered.

Luka nodded curtly and peered around at the fearful hunters and the small crowd of orphan children and teens. "You have nothing to fear from any of my people. They have strict instructions to leave you alone or lose their life!" Luka told them. "You can stay as long as you need."

A few people muttered their thanks, but I could

see their wary glances. They were without their leader, without their home, and in the hands of who they perceived as the enemy.

They needed Ruby.

"I've gotta bring Ruby back," I declared. "And while I'm at it, I might as well kill Maz."

Luka nodded. "I understand your anger, my love, but what if we tried a diplomatic solution first?"

I hated that he was babying me and my new emotions, but it was probably wise. I still felt slightly unhinged, like a bomb that could go off at any moment.

"Like what?" I growled.

"Like I, as the king of the vampires, promise not to attack the new fey breeder encampment they are most likely setting up if Maz gives us Ruby."

My mouth popped open. "You can't do that to those women, and what if it's not a new camp? It was just two women."

I knew everyone hated the Ithaki, but it wasn't fair that they just be left behind to become sex slaves and breeders.

Luka grinned, and holy hell it made my knees weak. "I didn't say I would honor it, Aspen. But it would buy us time."

Liv whistled low. "Promise not to attack and then attack. Sounds like the recipe for war."

Luka shrugged. "I have a responsibility as leader to set an example to all supernatural creatures. Sitting back while they kidnap, rape, and enslave women is not something I will be known for."

If I still had ovaries, they would be bursting right now.

"I love you," I blurted out, still unable to rein in my thoughts and feelings.

Luka grinned, pulling me toward him for a kiss as Vaz and Liv turned their heads to give us privacy.

After pressing my lips to his, I pulled back and I asked him to make the call and try to do the trade deal for Ruby.

He nodded. "You need to see your mother. She and Maple are worried sick."

Oh crap.

I'd grown up my entire life without a family. I wasn't used to having people rely on me. "I will, right after this."

He nodded. "I'll let you know what Maz says about the trade deal."

With a final kiss, he walked away and I spun to see Vasquez watching me.

"What? Totally weird, I'm engaged to a vampire right? I know. I—"

"No actually, I was just thinking how glad Sterling would be to know you'd moved on and found love and happiness," he said.

Emotion clogged my throat and I nodded, tears welling in my eyes. "Did you guys know I don't pee or poop anymore?" I said.

"TMI!" Liv plugged her ears, but Vasquez just grinned.

I stayed a few more minutes, talking to some of the others. Jason was Ruby's second-in-command, and I reassured him I was going to do everything possible to bring Ruby back. I sensed by the worried glances of the people that my presence was making them uncomfortable, so I headed over to my little cottage where my mother and Maple were waiting.

This wasn't going to be awkward at all...

"OH HEAVENS." My mom's hand went to her mouth when she saw me.

Maple's jaw unhinged. "You look *so* totally hot!" my half-sister said. "And you're going to be queen!

Does that make me a princess? Because I'm *totes* down for that."

My eyebrows drew together at her tween terminology. My mother shook her head. "She's been watching too much *Gossip Girl*."

Ahhh.

"That's dangerous," I told them both with a grin.

Maple smirked and stepped forward, reaching out to touch my hair. "Whoa, it's so soft. Can you hear my heartbeat?"

I focused on the sounds around me, and sure enough, there were two steady thumps in the room. "Yep."

"Does it hurt? Are you scared?" my mom asked, frowning.

I shook my head, stepping forward. "I'm fine. A little emotional, but totally fine."

My mom's gaze flicked to Maple. "Go play outside, honey."

She scowled. "But—"

"Go outside please." My mom's tone was in don't-mess-with-me territory.

Maple stomped off and slammed the door and my mom stepped right up into my space.

"How are you really? I heard you got shot and nearly died. Luka said to prepare for you not to make it." Her lip quivered. "I only just got you back. I wasn't ready to lose you again."

All of the memories of that night came rushing back. Morgana, the bullets tearing through my body, the bright light and weightless feeling of death.

My mom and I both broke down into tears as she reached out and pulled me into a hug. I'd never had this before, a mom, a person who loved me no matter what and would always worry about me. I should have come here first thing, I just hadn't been thinking. She must have been so concerned. "I'm okay now. I promise." I sniffled as she rubbed my back and pulled away to wipe her eyes.

"Well, you're a lot harder to kill now. At least that's something."

We both burst into laughter at that.

I looked at my mom and felt so much pride and respect for what she'd been through. "Mom, I have to tell you something."

She stiffened. "Okay."

I didn't want to, but she could be a valuable asset in our plan to save the women from these encampments.

"We found out some intel that there are more breeder camps in other magical enclave cities like

New York, Chicago..." I tapered off and waited for the reaction.

She frowned. "Wait, what?" Confusion crossed her face. I hated to be the one to bring trauma back into her life.

"There are six that we know of. The fey do it in every major city. It's a huge source of income for them."

Anger tightened her features. "Those baby stealing bastards!" she shouted suddenly, making me jump.

Whoa. *Go, Mom.*

"But don't worry," I told her. "We're going to free the women and close them all down."

How? I had no idea, but I wouldn't stop until it was done.

She nodded. "I will help if I can. I know how the Munai think, how the encampments are laid out, how the transactions work. All of it."

I grinned. "I was hoping you would say that."

A smile lit up her face. "Oh, Aspen, this would give me such a purpose. To help others. I'd be honored."

I nodded, glad that she was on board, but my mind was still playing out something she'd said. "Transactions?"

My mom bobbed her head. "They used to do them at the encampment, but after Olivia's mom ... well, now they don't make a scene. They take the baby the night before and meet up at a handoff place."

I raised one eyebrow. My mom had no idea what a wealth of information this was. "And where is that?"

My mom shrugged. "Changes. But they take someone with them, a breeder, so that we don't cause attention with the baby. Most of the fey have no idea where their government gets their money."

"Did they ever take you?" This was a gold mine of info I could relay to Demi and Sawyer if they were going to be looking further into the two women that got taken.

My mom nodded, a painful look crossing her face. "I was forced to pretend to be a baby's mother or they would hurt Maple."

My heart dropped at the sound of that. We definitely needed a therapist in Vampire City. "I'm so sorry." I reached out and grasped her hand, careful not to break it with my superhuman strength.

"Cold," she muttered, and I realized she meant my skin.

I gave a nervous laugh. "I am dead, you know."

She winced. "Don't say that."

It was true. "If I'm going to be a vampire, and the next vampire queen at that, I might as well use my power for good."

She nodded in agreement.

"I'm going to take the entire breeder program down across all six cities if it's the last thing I do."

My mom beamed up at me. "I would be so proud."

Leaning forward, she pulled me into a hug, and I left feeling lighter than I came. Moms were good at that. We dumped our stuff at their feet and they took it away.

I SPENT the rest of the afternoon feeling groggy and trying to get used to the new circadian rhythm of being a vampire. Luka had sent his demands to Maz through a messenger and also to the leader of the Dark Fey. The hours ticked by, him sitting in his office chair behind his desk reading papers, while I stared at my chest and freaked out that I wasn't breathing.

The knock came at the door and I bolted upright.

"Come in!" Luka said, and stood as his new

assistant, Austin, entered. This wasn't the type of negotiation you did over a cell phone apparently.

Austin bowed slightly, before standing to his full six-foot-four-inch height. "My King, I have your reply from Maz of the House of Rose."

Luka waved him on as if indicating he hurry up.

Austin cleared his throat, reaching up to rub the back of his neck nervously, and my heart plummeted.

"Sir, she said ... to go fuck yourself." He stood there frozen as if waiting for Luka to lash out at him. Meanwhile, all of my bottled-up rage for the woman who raised me popped its lid and exploded inside my chest.

"Thank you. You may leave," Luka said through gritted teeth.

The moment the door closed, I screamed, my yell turning to a growl of frustration. "That *bitch*! I'll disembowel her alive for this."

Luka's eyebrows raised and a slight grin pulled at his lips. "I kind of like this new Aspen."

I shook myself, clearly not fully over the emotions of the change. "So when do we attack?"

Luka sighed, slumping back into his chair. "*We* don't."

My jaw unhinged.

"Or *can't* rather," he quickly amended.

"Why not?" I growled. *Breathe. Don't kill him. He's really hot, and sweet most of the time.*

Luka stood, walking around the side of the desk to approach me. There was a mischievous look in his eyes. "As king of the vampires, I cannot be involved in any human business."

"Maz isn't human! She's a Munai!" I yelled.

He nodded. "One that's done nothing to me or my people, and Ruby is basically a human. If I lead a charge into Spokane, the Magical Creature Council will have my crown."

I fisted my hands. "Why didn't you tell me that before!?"

Luka was giving me a weird look, like I wasn't catching on to something. His eyes kept widening. "I hoped the political option would prevail. But now, since the truth witch with the Magical Creature Council will see everything, *I* cannot go."

Oh. *Oh.* Was he saying…?

I gave him a quizzical look. "What if *I* were to go?"

Luka had to force himself not to grin. "You are not my wife yet, so it would not affect my kingship, but I forbid it."

"I forbid it," was said with the same token as you

would tell someone to take out the trash. Luka knew that the truth witch might see this moment if this was investigated and he needed to look like he was not involved.

"Well, if you insist, then I will wait for another solution." I raised an eyebrow, hoping he was understanding me, because I was totally going to save Ruby.

He smiled, stepping forward and pressed his lips to mine. "I love you and I trust you to be safe and do the right thing."

Translation: Go get Ruby back and don't get killed...?

A slow grin pulled at my lips and I nodded.

We lingered there for a moment, not saying all the things we wanted to say for fear of the truth witch or whatever she was called being able to replay this moment. Could she hear us if we spoke into each other's minds? I just didn't know. What I did know was that I was a badass vampire now, full of rage, with emotion regulation issues, and I was going to get Ruby back, consequences be damned.

After leaving Luka's office, I popped over to my house to grab the papers Sterling had given me as evidence that the society hunters weren't human, and then went straight to Liv. She was outside the House of Thorn's barn talking to Vasquez and Jason.

"Maz declined the trade," I told them as they looked up upon my approach.

Vasquez growled, Liv cussed, and Jason looked livid. "So what now?" Jason asked.

"We run our own mission. Luka's forbidden it, but I'm going to go ahead anyway. I need ten of your best hunters. We leave in an hour," I told them.

The group whooped and cheered, and Vasquez and Jason disappeared inside to spread the news, but Liv stepped over to me.

"Hey, if Luka's forbidden you, are you sure you still wanna go? I can take lead—"

"I'm sure." I looked her in the eyes, hoping to convey that I had this handled. "Trust me."

The truth witch would see this moment too.

Her brows knotted in confusion, but she nodded. "Okay, then. Let's do this."

While the boys readied the hunting party, I went to the vampire armory and tossed around my engagement ring, telling them I was about to be their new queen and I desired Kevlar vests for eleven people, two duffle bags filled with weapons, and a fifteen passenger van. When one of them nodded and said they just needed to clear it with Luka, I told him that wasn't necessary. He looked mildly terrified of me, and I was sure he would call Luka the second I left, but that was okay. By then we would be gone, and Luka could pretend to be pissed, but he'd do nothing to retrieve the van, I was sure of it.

I gathered Jason and his crew of ten hunters, which included Vaz and Liv, and I shuffled everyone into the van. Once they were all in, I barreled out of Vampire City as fast as I could on the off chance I'd misread Luka and he really didn't want me to go. As we approached the gates leading out of the city, I slowed for the two guards.

The gates were closed.

Were they normally closed? I had no idea. I'd ram them if I had to. I rolled down my window when I recognized the lead guard as one of Luka's right-hand men. Diego, I think was his name.

"Miss Rose." He nodded and the gates opened.

Relief spread through me and I swallowed hard, returning the nod and passing through into the mortal world.

"So, what's the plan?" Jason asked from the back seat as our team suited up in Kevlar.

I'd been giving this a lot of thought. We could wait until Maz left the House of Rose building hoping to lure me into a fight ... or we could surprise her, flush her and everyone else out of the building and then get Ruby and scram before she had a chance to organize any type of attack.

"We start a fire, flush them out, and hope she brings Ruby when she evacuates."

Jason's eyes widened. "And if she doesn't?"

I nodded. "I'll go in and get Ruby out. I'm a vampire. Surely I can sustain some burns and heal."

Liv pulled a lighter from her pocket. "Want to test that theory right now?"

I rolled my eyes, getting onto the highway and heading for downtown Spokane. "No. It will be fine."

I was going to burn down the House of Rose.

No big deal.

ABOUT ONE HOUR, fifteen gallons of gas, and ten Molotov cocktails later, we arrived a block away from the House of Rose.

"Let's light this bitch up," Liv growled, double fisting the glass bottles full of gasoline. Long strips of cloth hung from the open mouth of the bottles.

I paused a second, thinking about the repercussions of what we were about to do. There were good people in there, good hunters who had no idea of Maz's dirty deeds. They were going to be heartbroken if this building went down—but if it meant saving babies from getting sold like slaves, then I'd do what I had to do.

"Liv, you still have that hunter email thread from last Christmas? The one we emailed behind Maz's back to set up that surprise for her?"

We normally all had hunter email addresses that ended with @HouseOfRose, but last year all of the hunters had needed to plan a surprise party for Maz and so we'd opened private emails. Something Maz would never see or track. I deleted everything. I hated if an email sat in my inbox for more than a few days, but Liv was an email hoarder.

"I think so yeah, but no phone or computer." She shrugged.

"Use mine." A Thorn hunter chick with short-cropped black hair handed Liv her phone.

Liv set the bottles down and grabbed the phone.

"Thanks." I smiled at the girl.

Not everyone had been cool with me when I first turned into a vampire, but it was nice to see at least one person warming up to the idea. Liv logged into her private account, pulling up the old chain email we'd done for Maz's Christmas surprise.

Bingo.

She handed me the phone and I hit reply all, but deleted Kenzley's and Finn's addresses because I wasn't sure I could trust them. Taking a deep breath, I started to type.

Dear fellow hunters,

You've all been lied to. I know this will be hard to believe, but Sterling died at the hands of none other than our fearless leader Maz. He died uncovering a great truth.

That truth is that we are not fully human.

We were stolen and paid for from our partially fey mothers all in an elaborate multimillion dollar scheme Maz designed.

Maz is a full blown fey and cares nothing for your welfare, only for the empire she's built.

You do not hunt vampires that are guilty of heinous crimes against humans. You weed out the vampire race for the highest bidders to line Maz's pockets. I have proof of everything attached.

Love,

Aspen and Liv

I pulled the papers Sterling had given me, including the personal letter he'd written me, and laid them on the dashboard, where I took some pictures of them. After attaching them all as evidence, I bit my lip and hit send.

"Let's do it." I didn't want to leave my fellow hunters in the dark. They'd read the email and maybe a few of them would break free from the hold Maz had over them.

I exited the van, allowing a tall and lanky male hunter to climb into the driver's seat. I couldn't remember his name, but he was now our getaway driver. I'd have to take time to get to know them all later on.

The second we were clear of the vehicle, he started to circle the block. Nearly a dozen hunters in Kevlar vests holding gas cans and Molotov cocktails were definitely going to attract unwanted attention, but there was nothing else we could do. I didn't want to do this at night and risk killing any hunters who were sleeping, because the sun didn't go down in the inland Northwest this time of year until past 9 p.m.

I looked up at the nondescript building as we approached and couldn't help but think of the karma we were about to dole out. Maz had burned House of Thorns, now we were going to take down House of Rose. The issue was, the bottom floor had no windows, only the front door, which was guarded at all times. If we wanted to light this place up, we'd need to get up to the second floor.

"Split into teams!" I whisper-screamed, having informed them on the drive over of what would need to be done.

The large male hunters spread out against the building about twenty feet apart, right under windows. They planted their feet and squatted. The next team were the lighter females. We gripped our Molotov cocktails and gas cans and climbed the men's backs like they were trees. Vasquez groaned as I planted a foot on his shoulder, but said nothing in the way of complaint.

His wrist came around my ankles to steady me and then he stood to his full height. It was just enough for me to reach the lower pane of the window. I smooshed the gas can between my chest and the building while I fumbled for my Glock. This floor was the one that held many rooms where there would be a lot of activity, so we'd need to act quickly. I looked to my left and right, confirming the rest of the hunters were in the same position as me, and with a nod I smashed the butt of my gun into the window, shattering it. Wasting no time, I holstered my gun and then grabbed the gas can, chucking it into the hole in the window, with no lid. I could hear the glug-glug of gas, along with some shouts of alarm from inside. Vasquez's arm came up holding a lit flame, and I tipped the end of the Molotov cocktail to it, igniting the cloth.

God forgive me. Don't let anyone innocent get hurt, I prayed, tossing the flaming bottle into the hole. The moment it hit the ground and shattered, it must have ignited the puddle of gasoline. There was a giant boom; the glass blew outward as I leapt from Vasquez's shoulders and landed on my feet.

Oh yeah. I was a vampire.

Shaking myself from my stupor, I helped Liv and some of the others down and we ran to hide on the side of the building, just as the bottom floor door burst open. The flames were already licking the outside walls of the second floor, and black smoke plumed high into the sky.

"Get in!" a voice called from behind, and I peered back to see our driver waiting with the van doors open. The plan was to get in the van and ride around the block a few times while everyone fled outside, but now I was wondering if I could use my new vampire abilities and jump to the third floor, above the fire. What if I could catch Maz coming out and make sure she had Ruby? What if Maz just left Ruby in there and she burned…?

"Go. I'll meet you at the pick-up location if we get split up," I whispered to Liv.

"What!?" she whisper-screamed. But it was too late, I was already running.

The one thing playing through my mind was how high Luka had jumped that night at the club when he'd saved my life by tucking me into the rafters with him. Could I jump that high? That was at least thirty feet, right?

"Aspen, don't you dare!" Liv's yell came from behind me, but I was already airborne. I burst off the ground with as much of a power jump as I could muster. I sailed through the air, approaching the building way faster than intended. Not only had I jumped superhumanly high, but also superhumanly fast.

"Crap," I muttered as I slammed into the brick wall between the third and fourth floor, cracking some of the bricks. Pain exploded in my wrists and feet as I started to drop.

Crap, crap, crap. As I fell past the third floor window, I hurled myself forward and crashed through the glass with zero finesse. My upper body made it through but my legs were halfway out the window, so they just dangled as I faceplanted onto the tile inside of the library.

"Ow," I whispered. Glass shards cut into my palms, but as quickly as the pain was there it vanished.

Vampy perk.

I rolled forward, lifting my dangling legs out from the window, and sprang to a standing position. I winced at the shrill shrieking of the fire alarm as it blared inside my brain with my super hearing. But it was good that the alarm went off. I hoped that was enough warning to get everyone out before the building went down. Following the sounds of screaming, I bolted for the door, on the hunt for Maz or Ruby.

We'd never kept prisoners before, but if we did I

would keep them someplace discreet, like the storage room where we kept the gym mats. Or maybe even one of the unused apartments depending how well I liked said prisoner. Considering Maz hated Ruby and seemed to only be keeping her alive for my benefit, I headed for the storage room.

The smoke was already billowing into this floor, and was it just me or did my feet feel hot?

Hunters ran in pandemonium down the side exit stairs, which had yet to become engulfed, and I had a moment of terror when I thought of the nursery on the fourth floor. They would get out in time, right? They had to ... or I'd never be able to live with myself. Maybe this had been a mistake ... maybe I should have called in a bomb threat first or something. We hadn't used enough gas to take the whole building down that quickly, it was just enough to scare them and flush them out ... right?

Now I was second-guessing this plan.

Cutting down the hall, passing a few hunters who barely looked my way, I found the storage closet locked.

Interesting, it was never locked before. That was a good sign that Ruby might be in here.

One hard twist of the knob and it came off right in my hand. I kicked the door wide and it splintered into four pieces.

Oops. Too much vampy mojo.

"Ruby!" I yelled.

A muffled scream came from deeper inside the room and I sighed in relief. Rushing in, with only the emergency lights to guide my way, I streaked past mats and old gym equipment. When I got to the back of the room, a whimper came to the right. Spinning, I saw Ruby chained to a radiator in the corner. She looked bloodied and bruised. Her hands were cuffed at an odd angle. Duct tape covered her mouth.

"Ruby!" I whizzed over to her and she froze.

Reaching out, I grabbed the chains with my bare hands and pulled. They strained against my strength for a split second, before buckling and tearing apart. Ruby's eyes went wide. I grabbed the corner of the duct tape next and pulled.

She winched as the tape ripped off and looked up at me in shock. "Aspen … you're a … *vampire.*"

I swallowed hard. "Yes. Long story, I almost died and it was necessary to save my life. The building is on fire. We need to scram."

She nodded, allowing me to help her into a standing position. "My hunters. The orphans."

"All safe in Vampire City. Ten of your best fighters are outside right now."

She sagged in relief against the wall, and I realized she had no intel this entire time and probably thought they'd all died.

"I'm way faster than you. Can I...?" I wrung my hands together in embarrassment. "Carry you?"

Ruby Thorn was my idol. If it was too demeaning for her, then—

"Hell yeah, piggyback me and let's blow this joint." She grinned.

I chuckled and turned to give her my back. Two seconds later, she'd latched on like a kid would, wrapping her hands loosely around my neck and shoulders. I was a blur of motion, zipping around the gym mats and through the now empty hall, which now plumed black smoke. By the time I reached the broken window I'd come in through, I'd only been running for seconds.

"That was kinda fun," Ruby said in my ear.

Well, she was taking the vampire thing surprisingly okay.

"Well, hold on tight, because this might *not* be fun," I told her, stepping out onto the ledge.

Looking down, I took in the scene below. A few dozen House of Rose hunters were bleeding out onto the side street, and the van was nowhere to be seen. I didn't recognize Maz, but she could be among them.

Ruby suddenly clenched my shoulders in a death grip. "Wait, you're not gonna jump, are you?"

Without waiting to give her an answer, I leapt into the pandemonium below.

"Shiiiiiit!" Ruby yelled all the way down. I landed with force jarring enough to dent asphalt, and pain shot up my calves. Ruby slipped off of me and stood at my side, trying to catch her breath.

The hunters on the street looked at us in shock as they coughed and panted, black soot marking their faces.

"Aspen!" Holly shouted.

"She's a vampire! Maz was right, she's with them," Anthony said, pointing at me.

"No, check your private email. The one we made for the Christmas surprise," Valerie said in my defense.

"I—" I'd barely had gotten a word out when the van screeched to a stop behind us. At the same time, Maz stepped out into the side alley.

Crap.

"Why does she have Ruby from House of Thorns?" Valerie asked.

I glared at my former mentor. "Because Maz was keeping her hostage."

Maz's face registered the slightest alarm at my new supernatural appearance before becoming a mask of calm. "You poor lost soul," she said to me. "You are so mad at my decision to kick you out based on your fornication with the undead that you would burn our building down?"

The hunters around her gasped.

"Aspen wouldn't do that," Valerie told them all.

Bless you, Val.

I chewed my lip.

I saw what Maz was doing. She wouldn't fight me in front of them and blow her cover, and if I took her head off right now, the hunters would gang up and kill me.

"Let's go!" Liv growled behind me from the open van doors.

"She burned House of Thorns!" I yelled, while backing into the van. "She kidnapped Ruby, hoping to lure me out."

Maz clicked her tongue, shaking her head. "Sweet child, we will pray for you and these lies that drip from your tongue so easily."

"But I saw her jump out the window with Ruby," Anthony muttered.

"Check your emails!" I said as I was yanked into the van by Liv. "I would never betray you guys!" Those were my last words as I fell into Liv's lap and the door slammed shut, the tires squealing on our escape.

"The nursery!" I yelped, looking back out the window. We were in the side alley, not the main frontage of the building, but I needed to know that they'd made it out.

"All the kids got out. We saw them when we circled the block," Liv assured me.

I collapsed in relief, but couldn't enjoy it fully. Maz had everyone under a spell, and she'd kept her cool so well I wasn't sure anyone was going to believe the email I'd sent. Technically, it could all be made up. I could have written that note from Sterling and made up the rest with a good computer program. The depression of that fully sank into my bones.

Ruby reached across the van and grasped my arm, pulling me from my thoughts. "Thank you for getting me out." Her team was hugging her and smiling ear to ear, but I just couldn't find the happiness. I wouldn't until Maz was dead and every single breeder was free.

'Hello, my love. Maz has just called in a complaint to the Magical Creature Council about a vampire attack. Where are you right now?' Luka's voice held amusement, but I knew we would have to play this off if we wanted his hands clean for the truth witch.

That evil witch Maz. Of course she would go running to the council the second I was gone. She was trying to do anything in her power to unseat Luka or throw me in jail.

'So you know that thing you forbade me to do?'

'Yes?' he replied knowingly.

'I did it,' I confessed.

'How dare you go against my word!' he shouted, jarring me. *'Anyone hurt?'* His voice was back to calm.

Now I wasn't sure if he was kidding or not. *'No.'*

'Good. See you at home soon. The truth witch will be waiting.'

Frick, already? I wasn't sure I was ready to see her, but I guessed it was better that she got in my head now and get it over with.

"What's up? You've got that look you get when you're talking to Luka," Liv asked as the van barreled down the highway toward the Idaho border.

I gave her a nervous laugh and looked at the

others. I didn't want them to feel guilty if I got in trouble for this. "Nothing. All good," I lied.

We drove the rest of the way in silence. All I could think about was the way my fellow hunters had looked at me with disgust.

"SHOULD I BE NERVOUS?" I asked Luka as we walked down the hall to meet the truth witch. She'd been kind-ish before, but I had no idea if what I'd done broke any supernatural laws.

Luka made a face that indicated he wasn't sure. "Technically you were a vampire when you burned down the building in Spokane, so you're now under supernatural law."

"Maz is a Munai!" I snapped.

Luka held out his hands. "We have no proof of that."

I chewed my lip and then a thought came to me. "Yes we do." I tapped my head. "The truth witch will see the attack at the cemetery if I tell her to look there, right?"

Luka bobbed his head up and down. "But she'll

64

also see you lighting fire to a building full of humans."

I scoffed. "They're Ithaki first of all, and I was saving Ruby's life!"

Luka nodded. "Let's see what she says." He stopped in front of the double doors and faced me. "I'm not permitted to go in this time."

I bobbed my head up and down and he leaned forward, pressing a kiss on my lips.

'If she sentences you to Magic City Prison, we'll run away together,' he said into my mind and I froze.

Magic City Prison?

I ... I was a vampire, so I guess that's where I would go. The shock of that was too crazy for me to process.

Oh man, I was not feeling this right now. I didn't regret what I'd done. Ruby was safe and with her people, and the resistance against the breeder farms would live on, but, man ... I was not cut out for prison.

I growled. "Let's just get this over with!" I snapped and spun around.

His arm snaked out and caught mine. "My love, when was the last time you fed?"

"This morning. Why?" My gaze flicked to his, daring him to say anything rude.

"Your eyes look a tad … cagey. Here, have this before you go in." Reaching into his pocket, he pulled out a bottle of blood.

Thirst flared to life. I snatched the bottle from him, bringing it to my lips. A moan ripped from my throat as the liquid chocolate poured down my throat. It. Was. So. Good. I mean, I would miss bacon, but this was second best.

Luka cleared his throat, adjusting the front of his pants. "When is our wedding night again. Can we set a date?"

He'd agreed to give me my dream wedding but that would take a bit of time to plan. Pulling the bottle from my lips, I grinned, licking my teeth. "A month? Gives us time to plan something nice."

He smiled and my heart melted. I loved that smile. "A month is perfect. My gift will be ready by then."

Gift. "Right. Mine too," I lied, and he only chuckled.

"Go on. Don't keep her waiting." He indicated the door and I nodded.

I stepped into the familiar space. The vampire council sat at the back of the room and dipped their heads in greeting as I approached.

Okay … didn't expect them to be here.

"We will bear witness. It's nice to see you in your eternal form, Aspen," the tallest one said.

Eternal form. Holy crap, what a reality check. I was going to live forever.

My gaze then fell on the truth witch. Her hood was pulled up and she looked road weary, with pale dry skin and messy hair. Probably had to travel here quickly for this issue.

I smiled. "Sorry for bringing you out here for this misunderstanding."

She raised one eyebrow. "I saw some very interesting video footage of you standing on someone's shoulders and setting a building full of humans on fire."

The elders gasped and I winced.

"I'll determine the misunderstanding," she added.

Crap. I cleared my throat and extended my hand. "But please go back further and look at the cemetery. Look at all of it," I pleaded.

She looked tired. Dark circles hung under her eyes, but she nodded in compliance. "Very well."

She grabbed my hand and the wall lit up with images. She'd gone way back as asked, unfortunately right to the spot where Morgana kidnapped me. I squeezed my eyes shut, not wanting to relive this, and she muttered an apology. "I'd like to see this too, for Morgana's sentencing when we catch her, if you don't mind. Otherwise, I'll need to come back and get your testimony..."

"It's fine," I told her, swallowing hard with my eyes still pinched shut.

Hearing Morgana speak out into the room made chills race up my arms, but I knew it was just from the memory and she wasn't here and couldn't hurt me. The thump of bullets unloading into my body made my stomach tighten and throb with phantom pain. The elders gasped at what they saw, but I kept my eyes closed.

"Evil woman," the truth witch muttered.

Luka's pleas to save me, along with Liv's, had tears running down my face. The truth witch squeezed my hand lightly. "I've seen enough of that for Morgana to be sentenced to death. Moving on," she told the room.

Sentence Morgana to death? That was a relief. I hoped I would be the one who could deliver such a sentence.

Next, I heard Liv and I at the cemetery and my eyes popped open. We were kneeling in front of Sterling's grave, and when I spun around I came face to face with Maz. The memory sped up until Maz dropped her illusion, then the truth witch's eyebrows raised.

"Interesting," she commented, as Maz showed her full-on Munai self.

That battle played out where I was shot yet again.

My poor body. Shot, my uterus carved out by Luka's former fiancée Cassara, shot again by Morgana. It was like I was destined to die.

When the witch got to the part where I was discussing Ruby with Luka, I froze.

"I forbid you to go," Luka's unconvincing voice rang throughout the room.

"There!" an elder vampire commented. "Our king is innocent in these matters."

The truth witch raised one eyebrow and went through the rest of the memories, including me burning down the building and saving Ruby. She saw Maz act all human in front of the other hunters, but also the email with the proof none of them were human.

By the time she was all caught up, she dropped my hand and stroked her chin.

"You're a supernatural now. You cannot put humans in danger," she scolded.

I swallowed hard. "Yes, ma'am."

"But…" She raised a finger. "I didn't see you come into contact with any humans. As far as I'm concerned, Maz is a Munai fey, and all of her hunters are Ithaki. You were just getting your kidnapped friend back after diplomacy failed. The Magical Creature Council will not be pressing charges."

I sagged in relief. "Thank you."

She nodded once, looking weary and ready for rest.

"Umm, can I ask you something?" I lowered my voice, although I was pretty sure the old geezers with super hearing could still hear me.

She tilted her head to one side, indicating I hurry.

"Are there any laws against going to other magical enclaves in other states?"

She seemed to consider my question. "If you can find them, there will be no quarrel with me or my council, but you might have an issue with whatever rules they have set up. We do not all run the same."

That was interesting. So each magic city had different rules? What if "kill all outsiders on sight" was a rule? I guess we were about to find out. Because we would need all the help we could get if we were to bring down the breeder camps in each city.

After thanking the witch and bowing awkwardly

to the council, which I'm pretty sure I wasn't supposed to do, I left and met Luka in the hallway.

He was smiling, standing super close to the door. "Went well?"

"You eavesdropped?" I assumed.

"Yep," he admitted.

A grin pulled at my face. I wrapped my arms around the back of his neck. "Luka, what if I put my mom and Maple in charge of wedding planning and we take a trip to LA? Meet with the vampires there and see if they can help us."

Luka's eyebrows raised. "Other magic cities are not like ours. Los Angeles might be a war zone with vampires as slaves for all we know. We could be walking into a death trap."

I nodded. He was king, he had to worry about leaving his people without a leader. "I understand. I'll take Liv, we can be back in two days—"

He looked at me like I'd grown a second head. "Are you crazy? I'm not letting you go alone."

"Luka, there are at least six other breeding programs throughout the United States. We need help taking them all down at once so they can't rebuild. These other magic cities might not even know about them—women and children in slavery."

He sighed. "Well, we can't have that, can we?"

"Eeeeee," I squealed, and popped on my tiptoes to press my lips to his. When we parted, his tongue stroked mine and a delicious heat shot down my body. Luka's hands grasped my hips and squeezed as a low moan rumbled in my throat.

Pulling away, he looked down at me with hungry eyes. "So, a month? Are we setting a date?"

My head tipped backward and laughter pealed out of me. I think Luka was having a little problem with my saving myself for marriage. "A month from today. I'd like to find a holy person to marry us—"

"I've got that covered." He brushed me off. "It will be your dream wedding. Just have your mom and Maple work on decorations with my new assistant, Austin."

I smiled, beaming ear to ear. I could feel my old self returning, the emotional instability and inner turmoil receding. "I love you, Luka Drake."

"And I you, Aspen soon to be Drake. Or Rose. Whatever you want."

"Aspen Drake has a nice ring to it," I admitted.

With that, we walked hand in hand out into the garden to plan our trip to Los Angeles.

"BRO, THIS IS CRAZY." Sawyer rubbed the scruff at his chin. The big alpha was standing next to his wife, who nodded in agreement. We were all in Luka's wing of the castle, standing in the giant living room. I still got lost in the palace. It would take me time to get used to it.

"The vampires in Los Angeles could be cannibals for all you know," Demi warned.

I snickered. "I'm pretty sure it doesn't work that way. Besides, there are women and children trapped there. I have it on good authority."

Ruby had intel on LA, New York City, New Orleans, Austin, Chicago, and Minneapolis. All six of the magical enclaves there were wiring money to some faction of the society. Fifty grand at a time. Since Los Angeles was the closest city, we figured we could start there and put out some feelers.

Sawyer rubbed the back of his neck. "Look, no offense, but no one present grew up here but me." He gestured to Demi, Luka, and me. "My dad told me some horror stories about the other enclaves. Some of them aren't segregated between the magical races. They constantly brawl in the streets over race wars. He even said there was a rumor that the fey rule most of the enclaves in other cities and the vampires and werewolves pay a tax to them to be allowed to remain living there."

Luka, Demi and I gasped at the same time.

"So you're saying our people could be enslaved in one of these other cities as well? Are there Paladin wolves there?" Demi asked.

Sawyer looked like he regretted saying so much. "I dunno, babe. I was like eight years old when he told me this. He had a map—"

"A map you say?" I moved closer to Sawyer with one eyebrow raised and Demi grinned for a second before her face fell. "You still have that map? Or was it lost when the house was destroyed in the war?"

Damn. That sucked.

Sawyer growled, "It's in the safe deposit box with the rest of my inheritance, but Demi—"

"Oh, perfect, let's go to the bank and get it." She grabbed her car keys from the counter and shook them.

It was very clear that what Demi wanted, Demi got.

"Fine, but this doesn't mean we're going with them. We have a son and this is a suicide mission," Sawyer told his wife.

She nodded absentmindedly, but I knew that if she did decide to go with us, nothing would stop her.

IT WAS a short drive to Werewolf City, where Demi parked her SUV downtown at Hudson Bank.

"Bank has your last name on it. Coincidence?" I asked Sawyer.

"Nope." Demi popped the P and I chuckled.

What did it feel like to be that rich? I would certainly never know. Maz stole all of my money, and I was sure there was some royal prenup I would be asked to sign before our wedding day. As long as I had a roof over my head and food in my belly, I was happy to sign whatever was needed.

A female bank teller leapt from behind her desk to greet the alphas as we stepped inside. "Hello, Mr. and Mrs. Hudson!"

Sawyer nodded his head to her. "Hi, Stacy, I'll need access to my safe deposit box."

She bobbed her head up and down and then scurried off to grab some keys from a drawer. When she returned, we followed her to the back of the room, where a solid steel vault door stood. "Finger." She indicated that Sawyer touch the keypad to the right of the door. He placed his thumb on it and then she inserted a key next to it. There was a beep, and then a hiss as the door opened.

When it did, my jaw dropped. The entire room was filled with papers, old leatherbound books, jewelry, bars of gold, and stacks of silver coins.

"Wait, this entire room is your safe deposit box?" Demi asked. She must have never been here.

Sawyer blushed a bit. "Yeah."

His wife snickered. "You're stupid rich."

The alpha shrugged. "Well, you're married to me, so you're stupid rich too."

She spit her tongue out at him and grinned. "I'm going to get that on a shirt," she said.

Stacy left us, and our little group stepped into the room.

"Holy crap, a tiara!" Demi grabbed the diamond studded piece. It was breathtaking. There was a giant ruby in the center of the crown that matched my engagement ring.

"Gift to my great grandmother on her wedding night," Sawyer told his wife. Demi placed it on her head as the men stepped deeper into the room to look at the old papers.

Demi and I gawked at the jewelry. "This would look amazing with your red hair. Try it on," Demi said, pulling the tiara off and placing it on me.

I laughed, feeling giddy at the weight of the crown on my head.

"Fit for a queen." Luka glanced at me and I suddenly felt shy. Reaching up, I took it off and set it back in its case. Demi squealed when she saw a set of baby blue aquamarine earrings. "OhmyGawd, Sawyer, I *need* these." She pulled the backs off and tried them on.

I burst into laughter at her excitement. Sawyer just gave his wife an endearing look. "Then they are yours, my love."

"Your mom won't care?" she asked tentatively, fingers twitching over the gems that now glittered on her lobes.

He shook his head. "She has her own vault. This is all the stuff they left for me and my future heirs and wife."

Demi's eyes bugged, then she looked over at me. "Stupid rich," she mouthed, causing me to grin.

I liked her. I liked Sawyer. Holy crap, I was a vampire who was close friends with two were-wolves. *Is this real life?*

Demi and I ransacked the jewelry, trying it all on and parading around in it while the boys painstakingly looked for that map.

"Oh, this would be perfect for Sage's wedding!" Demi's hand stilled on an emerald green necklace and earring set.

"Totally," I agreed.

"Babe?" Demi asked.

Sawyer parroted the same thing he'd been telling her over the past hour: "Take whatever you want, my love, you don't need to keep asking."

Demi grinned.

"Are you this rich?" I asked Luka jokingly.

He and Sawyer shared a look, causing both to grin.

"He's richer," Sawyer admitted, and my stomach dropped out.

Wait, what? I was kidding.

"Living forever means we have a lot of time to ... secure our wealth," Luka told us. "All vampires pay a crown tax, and the reigning Drake gets the honey pot, so to speak."

"Okaaay, girl, *damn*," Demi whispered and I just snort-laughed.

Luka's money was not my money and never would be. I liked to make my own way.

"Got it!" Sawyer shouted.

We scrambled from our seat at the jewelry stash and peered over Sawyer's shoulder.

Chicago, New York, New Orleans, Los Angeles, Austin, and Minneapolis! The six cities that Ruby had told me she had confirmed deposits from all had stars over them. The one marked Los Angeles was a green star.

At the bottom of the map, next to the key, the green star said: *Spicy Pho City.*

We all frowned.

Red star over Austin Texas said: *Vegan Barbeque.*

"They're restaurants," Demi mused.

"Entrances to the enclaves?" I wondered aloud.

"That's what my dad made it seem like. It's not like here where you can just drive in. He said the entrances were small, exclusive, and closely monitored. Something like that."

I pulled out my burner flip phone and took a picture of the map. "Thank you, this is super helpful."

Demi looked at my flip phone in disgust. "Luka, you need to get your woman a better phone."

Luka grinned. "It's on the to do list."

I turned to my fiancé. "It looks like I'm hungry for pho. How about you?"

Luka took in a deep, fake, unnecessary breath. "Let me at least tell the council, so if we wind up missing they know where to look for my dead body. We can leave first thing tomorrow."

"Not funny!" I smacked his firm pecs. "It's going

to be great. You and the vampire king of Los Angeles will probably be besties."

Sawyer frowned. "If you don't call me in twenty-four hours, I'm sending in the troops."

Demi nodded. "And once you find out about the breeder camp, we'd love to help with the attack."

"We would?" Sawyer asked his wife. "Another one?"

"We *would*," she pressed.

"Yes. We would," Sawyer confirmed.

Luka clapped Sawyer on the back and pulled him into a bro hug. "Instead, how about you keep your eye on the fey for me here. I might need you to help secure the home front while we deal with the breeder issue."

Sawyer nodded. "Now *that* I can do."

I gave Demi a quick hug and thanked them both again before Luka and I stepped outside, where his new assistant was waiting in a black SUV.

"What if the vampire council says no?" I asked.

He shrugged. "I'm not asking permission. I'm just telling them."

I loved this man.

Tomorrow we would be entering a whole new world, literally, and I'd be lying if I said I wasn't nervous.

WE HAD no way of knowing if Ithaki or humans were even allowed in this mysterious Los Angeles magical enclave, so we felt it best for Luka and I to travel there alone. Ruby and Liv begged to tag along, but we couldn't risk it. This was a scouting mission only. We would report back and make a gameplan from there.

I drummed my fingernails on the pull-down tray of the Drake family private jet as we flew to Los Angeles. "Any word on Morgana's whereabouts?"

Luka's jaw ticked. "No. She's completely gone off grid. Not hanging at any of her usual haunts, her cell phone was deactivated, and her summer house in Coeur d'Alene is empty."

She must have gotten quick word that I'd been changed and Luka was seeking revenge.

"Well, the truth witch let slip that based on what she saw, it was good enough for a death sentence," I told him.

Luka's head swiveled to mine. "One I will inflict very slowly upon her."

A frown pulled at my lips. "What about the Sire-Fledgling Pact? It seemed like a big deal at the fight."

"Screw the pact! She nearly killed my wife!" Luka screamed so loudly the vampire air hostess shot him a quizzical look.

"Luka." I lowered my voice. "*I* want to kill her."

"No," he growled, the veins in his neck twitching. "I will do it."

"And what happens to your crown if you break that pact?" I asked.

Reaching out, he grasped my left hand, fingering the engagement ring on my finger. "Aspen … I care more for revenge and your honor than I do about my position as king. I will take care of Morgana or I will never be able to proudly call myself your husband."

His tone was final. The king had spoken. And although his words were harsh, they were also sweet. I'd have to let it go, for now.

When we landed at LAX, there was a hired car ready to take us to Spicy Pho City in Burbank. This plan was kind of crazy but I didn't see any other way to learn about what was going on inside these other enclaves than to visit them ourselves. My stomach was tied into knots as I tried to act human around the other people at the airport. Even though it was a private plane and we were able to disembark at a smaller terminal, there were humans and I could hear their heartbeats, smell their coppery chocolate blood pulsing in their veins, and sense when they were staring at Luka and I.

"People are staring," I hissed, trying to remember to walk slowly and fake breathe.

Luka chuckled. "Because we're both really good looking."

I glared at my man. "Well, at least one of us is humble."

He reached over and slung his arm around my waist, giving me a wink that made my immortal knees go weak.

IT WAS a short drive to the pho shop, which was in a little nondescript strip mall. Definitely not the place where you would expect to find an entrance into a magical world. Luka thanked the driver and paid him as we grabbed our backpacks with a change of clothes and bottled blood on ice. We were hoping to only be here a couple hours, maybe one night at most. I still hadn't drank from a live person and I was going to keep it that way forever if I could. Luka was drinking "dead blood" in solidarity with me. We stepped to the curb, looking at the frontage of the building for any indication this was some supernatural building, but all I saw were a few people eating from steaming hot bowls by the window, and a sign that read *Extra Spicy*.

We had just stepped onto the sidewalk and Luka was about to open the door when I heard someone trying to get my attention.

"Pssst!" they hissed behind us.

I spun, and when my gaze landed on Liv and Ruby peeking out from the side of the building, I nearly fainted.

"What the hell are they doing here!?" Luka hissed.

We pivoted and hauled butt in their direction. I was hoping Liv could read the look of anger on my face, because the fact that they'd come here after we told them not to was *so* incredibly stupid.

"Talk," Luka growled at them.

Liv winced, looking at Ruby as we stepped into the side alley.

"We want to come too. You'll need more eyes—" Liv started.

Luka cut her off. "We've talked about this. We don't know their views on Ithaki—"

Now it was Liv's turn to cut him off. "We are *basically* human. You couldn't even tell Aspen was part fey. We'll pose as your feeders. Vampires need those, right? Perfectly reasonable explanation."

Luka growled and looked at me.

I stared at my bestie. "We don't want you guys to get hurt. We're vampires..." I lowered my voice to a whisper. "We can handle ourselves, but if we are separated..."

Ruby laughed, actually tipped her head back and laughed. "Aspen Rose, I will forgive that comment this once. You of all people know what hunters are capable of."

Damn. She was right. When I was human, I had hated when Luka treated me so fragile. Hunters took down vampires. They were more than capable. Shame burned inside of me.

"I mean, it would be nice to have a second set of hands in case we need to split up and scout the area," I told Luka.

He threw his hands up in exasperation. "They're

your friends. If they want to risk it..." He shrugged his shoulders.

I nodded, turning to face the girls. "Not a word of who Luka really is. We are posing as traveling vamps looking for a place to stay as we move to New York City," I told them.

They nodded, looking excited that we were going to allow them along.

"You're not carrying any weapons, right?" Luka asked them.

Both girls looked at each other guiltily and Luka rolled his eyes. "Stash them behind the trash can," he growled. "Feeders don't walk around with stakes in their waistbands!"

Liv and Ruby ran over to the restaurant's big industrial trash can and tossed their weapons behind it before joining us back on the sidewalk.

"I will lead the conversations," Luka informed us.

I nodded, fine with that. I hadn't been a vamp long enough to know the ins and outs, especially not in a new world.

We took off down the sidewalk and back to the pho restaurant. This time, we stepped inside and I was hit with the scent of salty broth and smoky meat. Not nearly as mouthwatering as it would have been to me months ago.

"Hello!" a short woman with black hair tied into a bun said as we approached the counter. My gaze flitted about the room, taking in everything and looking for any sign of anything supernatural. The couple eating seemed human to me and my nose. There was a door that led back to the kitchen that could conceal something I guess, but other than that—

Oh, the woman. The woman had pointed fey ears.

"Greetings." Luka smiled, flashing his canines.

The woman raised one eyebrow and glanced at the human couple eating. "Can I help you?"

Luka nodded. "My fiancée and our ... *dinner companions* ... are traveling to New York and looking for a *magical* place to stay overnight."

Why couldn't we just fly to New York like normal people? I didn't know, but she didn't seem bothered enough to question it.

"Four people, that's a four hundred dollar entrance fee." She rang up something on her register and then held out a credit card chip reader to him.

A hundred dollars just to enter the magic city? Wow.

Luka pulled out his credit card, not missing a beat, and swiped it. It beeped, printing out a receipt, and she handed it to Luka. The fey then pointed to the door that led back to the kitchen.

Holy crap, we'd actually found the entrance to another magic city. I didn't know whether to be scared or excited.

Luka gave the fey a curt nod, then we all stepped over to the kitchen door marked *Private.* Luka pushed it open and we stepped inside, but it wasn't the kitchen at all, it was a hallway. The kitchen was smaller than it appeared, which left room for this extra space.

At the end of the hallway there was a—I inhaled through my nose—witch, sitting on a stool in front of another nondescript door. She looked young, like us, early twenties, and wore skinny jeans with a black lace top. Her arms were covered in sleeves of skull and rose tattoos, and her hair was dyed cotton candy pink and pulled into a top knot.

She looked up as we approached and her nostrils flared. I'd learned two things already. In this magical world, the fey and witches were working together.

"Hello, darlings." She reached out a hand for the receipt Luka held.

"Good evening." Luka bowed formally to her and handed her the paper.

She snort-laughed, taking the paper from him and glancing down at it.

She brushed her hand over the knob of the door and it glowed with a golden fire. "Welcome to Night City. Have fun." She winked.

Night City? I took mental note of that so we could write it down later and start to map all of this out. Luka opened the door handle and pushed it wide. Stepping inside, I followed him, making sure Liv and Ruby were right behind us, and realized we were in a dark, stone hallway.

"Let's keep moving." Luka's voice sounded strained. I knew he didn't like going somewhere that he didn't know everything about, and to be honest I was a bit worried too. We walked quietly down the stone hallway and I stared at the dimly lit wall torches that didn't look like real fire. They glowed a sickly green.

Magic?

There were noises up ahead and we picked up the pace. I could see blurs of people passing under a streetlight. Luka blocked my view momentarily before stepping out into a bustling street. I was next, nearly running into his back because he had stopped so abruptly, staring at something.

"What?" I asked, and then fell silent when I saw

the fey woman walking down the street with a large dog attached to a collar and leash.

'That's not a dog,' Luka's sickened voice came through our bond.

Oh.

Oh crap. It was a werewolf. We were in a world where werewolves were second class citizens. Demi was not going to like hearing about that.

We were on a small side street bustling with shops. I skimmed the signs that hung above the doors. *Regina's Crystal Shop, Devil's Brewery, Dragontails Book Stop, Bloody Valentine Candy Shop.*

Luka pointed to Bloody Valentine and started walking in that direction. Seemed vampy. Might be our best shot.

"Bloody Valentine Candy Shop?" I muttered to Liv. "Someone needs to work on their marketing." She snickered.

I wasn't paying attention when I turned back, so I slammed right into the chest of some girl.

"Ohhfh," I yelped as she crashed against me.

I pulled back and was met with the terrified gaze of a redheaded female troll.

"Madam." She fell to my feet, touching my toes with her fingers. "Forgive me. I wasn't watching where I was going." Her voice broke; she sounded on the verge of a sob.

I froze, confused.

People stopped what they were doing and took notice of the scene.

"It's fine, I was the one—" I started, then a female vampire stepped over to me. She held her chin high, long glossy black hair flowing down her back.

"Did she hurt you? I will take her to the magistrate for sentencing." The woman lunged forward and grasped the troll girl's wrist, yanking her up to her feet. A sob ripped from the girl's throat and she whimpered. I noticed now, when I looked closer, that the troll girl had a silver collar on, much like the ones Demi wore on her wrist to keep her powers at bay.

"No. Hey, this is a big misunder—" I started when Luka stopped me.

"What my fiancée means is, we prefer to do our punishing in private." He winked at the vampire, whose eyes hooded as she raked her gaze over him.

Bitch, he's taken, I wanted to say, but controlled my temper.

Trolls and werewolves were inferior to vampires here, that much was clear. I didn't want this poor girl going to prison for something as stupid as bumping into me.

"Exactly," I said, and yanked the girl's wrist away from the female vamp.

The vampire looked at me suspiciously and I noticed the surrounding crowd had gotten bigger. I reached over and ran a finger along the girl's throat. "She would look nice in a pink collar. Don't you think so, honey?" I asked Luka, and the female vampire burst into laughter along with the vampires, witches, and fey in the crowd.

Luka smiled, but it didn't reach his eyes. The vampire woman nodded, then left, and the crowd broke apart.

"Change of plans," Luka said, and pointed to a hotel at the end of the block. "Let's go there and get a room."

'Too many supernatural ears here,' he told me through our bond.

I nodded.

The girl shook like a leaf in my arms. "Please, I ... I have a family. I was so stupid not to see you. I'm sorry."

"Shh," I told her, and lightened my grip. I could say nothing more until we were alone.

Liv and Ruby wisely kept their heads down. I had yet to see one human or Ithaki.

Dragging the shaking troll along, I followed Luka to The Broken Moon Resort. The door handles were crescent moons and I was hoping that meant this place was run by werewolves, who I'd trust a whole lot more than my own kind in this new place.

I'd been asking myself something since we walked through that door in the pho restaurant: did we walk into a portal? Because there was no way this was Burbank, CA. anymore.

Luka quickly bought two adjoining rooms from a nice werewolf woman who I was saddened to see wore a neck collar much like the troll's, which I was pretty sure kept her from shifting.

The troll woman kept mumbling apologies, and I felt awful that I couldn't yet reassure her that we wouldn't kill her or whatever the punishment was for bumping into a vampire. We passed a few fey in the hallway who gave polite nods, and then a vampire with one human feeder on each arm who nodded to Liv and Ruby. By the time we reached our room, I had more questions than answers. We all shuffled inside, the poor troll sobbing now, and the second the door shut, I spun on her.

"I'm not going to hurt you!" I blurted out. "We are

visiting from another city. We like trolls where we come from."

The girl froze, cheeks wet with tears as she looked up at me open mouthed. "What?"

She wore a dirty apron over an ankle-length skirt. There was grease under her fingernails and she looked underfed. My protective instinct went into overdrive. She was maybe twenty years old. The hard lines around her eyes told me she'd seen some rough days.

Luka stepped around me to face the girl, while Liv and Ruby sat on the bed.

"We're from a magic city enclave in Idaho. Trolls have their own city there and are a well-respected people."

The girl didn't say a word, she just swallowed hard, looking at us both like we were crazy. The tusks in her cheeks twitched. "*Other* magic cities?" she finally said.

Ahhh, so she was as clueless about other magic cities as we were until recently.

I nodded. "There are at least seven that we know of. Chicago, New York, New Orleans, Los Angeles, Austin, Minneapolis, and of course Idaho, where we are from."

She shook her head. "I ... why are you here?"

Luka nodded. "I'm hoping that if we tell you, then you can help us, and in turn we might be able to help you too?"

She rung her hands nervously. "Is this a trick? You're vampires. Of course I will do anything you say and without requiring anything in return." Her gaze fixated on the floor.

This world had broken her and that made me so mad. I could feel my unstable emotions rising to the surface, but I swallowed them down. I didn't want to scare this girl, but I wanted to bash someone's head in for what they'd done to her, to make her so afraid.

"Do you like werewolves? I mean, are you friendly with them?" I asked.

She nodded. "Of course." Right, because they were both slaves here.

"If you help us, we will bring you back to Idaho with us where you can live with another troll friend of ours. Her name is Marmal and she's in a wolf pack."

Her chin tipped upward and her eyes went wide as she gawked at me. "Wolf packs are forbidden." Then she smiled lightly, brushing the dust from her apron. "My grandmother's name was Marmal. We called her Marmie."

"Where we come from, wolves and trolls are

powerful people. If you help us, we will take you with us," I promised.

Luka's gaze flicked to mine as if asking *"What are you doing, woman?"* But I ignored it. We could cover her tusks with a scarf, and we were going on a private plane anyway. I was *not* leaving this girl here.

"I will help you." She grinned, showing a few missing teeth. This girl had a hard life. I just couldn't leave her here to continue that.

What was one more woman to break out?

WE SPENT the next hour talking with the troll. We'd learned her name was Milika, and we told her things on a need-to-know basis only. She didn't know Luka was royalty or that I was newly changed, or that the girls were vampire hunters. But when we described fey encampments that forced pregnant women to sell their babies, her entire body went rigid. She stared at the floor and said nothing, picking at her nails. We told her there was the same type of encampment in Idaho, but that we'd attacked it and freed the women.

She gasped. "You *attacked* the fey? But what about the alliance?"

"We have no alliance with the fey where we're from," I told her for the fifth time.

Poor thing was taking in a lot of information all at once.

"Do you know about these breeder camps? Do you have one here?" I urged her.

She chewed her bottom lip. "This is a trick. I tell you and then you imprison me." She crossed her arms and looked to the sky in defiance.

I groaned, looking at Luka. "Can I borrow your phone? Video chat Demi for me."

He raised one eyebrow but complied. Pulling out his phone, he video chatted Demi and handed the phone to me.

When Demi picked up, I could see the Paladin village behind her. "Hey, Aspen. How's it going?" she asked.

Milika leaned forward, spellbound by the phone, as if she'd never seen one.

"We've hit a snag. I was wondering if we could talk to Marmal?"

Demi looked over my shoulder, probably at Milika, and nodded, starting to jog. "She's at the barn."

Within seconds, thanks to her werewolf speed, Demi was at the barn. "Marmal!" she yelled for the troll.

Milika sniffed the phone, as if trying to tell what race Demi was through the device.

"Wolf. Alpha," I told her.

She stayed silent until Marmal's face suddenly came into view. "Hey." Marmal smiled, her tusks dipping into her cheeks.

How did I explain all of this to Marmal while Milika was right here? "Hey, we're in a magic city in Los Angeles and the trolls here are … not treated very well."

Marmal frowned and nodded to Milika before opening her mouth and speaking in a totally foreign language.

Milika bounced on the edge of the bed in surprise, rattling off a response in the same language and laughing.

Okay…

"What did she say?" I asked Milika. Trolls must have a special language. I never knew that.

"She says trolls are treated good where she is and the alpha is nice, except for her obsession with phones and technology, which are evil."

"Hey!" Demi's voice could be heard off camera and we all laughed, lightening the mood a little.

Marmal said something else and Milika spoke right back in rapid-fire troll language. It was fascinating, and I allowed them to talk for however long they needed, until finally the conversation wound down.

Milika pulled away and handed the phone back to me. "Thanks," I told her and stood, walking into the bathroom with Marmal still on the line.

I shut the door behind me, leaving Luka, Milika, Liv, and Ruby in the room, and flicked on the fan. "I'm alone now. So, what's up? What did she say?"

Marmal's tusks turned down as she frowned. "It's bad there. Nothing like here. The trolls and were-wolves are slaves—"

"WHAT!" Demi screamed from somewhere behind Marmal.

"Shh," Marmal shushed her friend and kept going. "Witches, vampires and fey run the world. Trolls and wolves are treated like rats and dogs."

"Those mother fu—" Demi started.

"She also said that the baby selling house is a brothel," Marmal added, and my stomach dropped.

I swallowed hard. "What do you mean?"

"Humans who know about the supernatural world pay to have sex with these women who are chosen as they have a small amount of fey genetics and are mostly human. When they get pregnant, the guy has no idea, and the baby is sold to the Los

Angeles Vampire Hunter Society ... among other places."

I might not be a mother—hell, I didn't even have a womb anymore, but the words *selling babies* made anger flush through me so fast and hot that I cracked the phone screen.

"Is she sure about all this?" I pressed Marmal through gritted teeth.

Our troll friend nodded. "She is a maid at the brothel. The front is a ... whorehouse. The back is where they hide the pregnant women and birthing mothers until they can sell the merchandise. Her words, not mine."

Sex slavery. This was freaking sex slavery. I mean, you read about it on the news in other countries, but...

There was a knock at the hotel door and I froze. "Call you later," I whispered, and hung up, slipping Luka's phone into my pocket.

Luka was up and across the room in seconds, and I was by his side. If vampires were the big dogs in this city, then Luka and I needed to use that to protect the others in our group who were looked down upon.

Luka pulled the door back to reveal a petite vampire woman with long black hair. She was holding a white envelope.

"Mr. Drake?" she asked.

I froze. They knew his name?

Luka played it off casually. "And who are you?"

She smiled. "My name is Carmen, assistant to King Constantine. He heard that a Drake used their credit card to buy tickets into Night City and now he must have you and your fiancée for dinner."

Dinner with the freaking king? So much for laying low.

How did the king even know that the Drake name was important or that I was his fiancée?

Luka beamed. "Oh, that would be wonderful. Is that the invitation?"

She handed it over, looking Luka up and down in a way that made jealousy spring to life within me again. An involuntary growl rumbled in my throat and the woman looked at me with surprise.

"My beautiful wife-to-be is newly changed and still learning to regulate the emotions," Luka interjected.

Understanding crossed Carmen's face and she took a step backward. "So we will see you tonight?"

"We wouldn't miss it," Luka told her, and she nodded once more before leaving.

Luka shut the door then and faced me.

My teeth clanged shut with anger. "Talk about my emotion regulation *one* … more … time … and see what happens." I glared at him.

He leaned forward and kissed my cheek. "I love you. Let's open this, shall we?"

I groaned. "Fine."

We brought the letter over to where Liv, Ruby, and Milika were hiding behind one of the beds. "It's safe to come out," I told them. "Just a dinner invite from the king." My voice was laced with sarcasm.

Milika's hands went to her mouth. "King Constantine wants to meet you?"

"Tell me everything you can about him," Luka urged her.

The troll folded her hands in her lap and looked at the ground. "He's … vile. Evil. You should not go."

Luka and I both frowned at her assessment of him. "I don't see how I can miss it. Can you tell me more about him so that Aspen and I can be prepared?" Luka urged her.

Milika nodded, resigned. "He is a purist. Vampire, fey, and witch only. Everyone else is beneath him. Mixes are not allowed—"

"Not allowed how?" I asked her.

"They are killed or sold, depending upon the pedigree," she replied blankly.

Liv, Ruby, and I all froze, processing without going into a cussing fit and scaring her. The Ithaki were killed or sold? Those were the only options? And since when was being a big badass werewolf the bottom of the food chain?

"What else?" Luka pressed her.

"He holds the Freedom Games every year," she said.

"What's that?" he asked.

"Slaves enter in a fight to the death, and the last one standing gets to be free, no collar. This year's fight is next week."

I glared at Luka. "That sounds familiar." Those stupid vampire king crowning fights were just as barbaric.

"Is he married?" I asked her, wondering what type of conversation I would have to uphold with the woman of the house.

"He was. She's dead." Milika's eyes hit the ground again.

Luka and I shared a look of dismay. "How did she die?" I asked.

Milika swallowed hard. "He killed her three years ago for having an affair with a werewolf."

Yikes.

"The psycho killed his own wife?" Ruby blurted,

and then started to pace. I knew we were all thinking the same thing. Save the wolves. Save the babies. Save the trolls. Kill this king. But it just couldn't happen. Not today, probably not even this year. This kind of culture needed to be systematically dismantled. But we could start with the babies and the women in the brothel. Put an end to that.

"He didn't kill her at first, just cut out her tongue," she said flatly.

Nausea rushed through my system and I looked at Luka. "We're in hell. This is literal hell."

He nodded. "Maybe we should go. Let—"

I put one hand on my hip. "Let babies be killed or sold based on their pedigree? Are you crazy? That is not the man I'm going to marry."

He pinched the bridge of his nose. "Okay, but we can't do this alone, and my most powerful allies, Sawyer and Demi, are dogs to these people, so what do you want from me?"

He was right. We needed help. We couldn't barge in here with a small group and get all those women and children out. This place was too well locked down.

"Is the pho shop the only entrance and exit?" I looked to Milika.

Milika looked confused, and I realized she'd

probably never left this place. "How many exits into the real world are there?"

She nodded in understanding then. "Three."

"Can you draw me a map?" I grabbed the hotel notepad and pen.

"What are you thinking?" Luka asked.

"I'm thinking we need to go to the dinner with the king tonight, and get an invite to the Freedom Games. Us and a dozen of our vampires, a bonding of our two peoples."

Luka grinned. "That's genius. And then while the games are going on, our teams will attack, get all the women and children out."

I bobbed my head in agreement.

"I hate to be the bearer of bad news," Ruby said, "but if we really want to do this and bring it all down, we need to hit up the other five cities at the same time."

She was right. A coordinated attack was best. "Okay, you are basically worthless here, no offense. Why don't you and Liv go to Austin, send Demi and Sawyer to New Orleans, Vaz and Jason to NYC, Sage and Walsh to Chicago, and Marmal and Rab to Minneapolis. Do recon missions only, try not to be seen you have no idea if your race is even welcome in other cities."

"It's a good idea," Ruby agreed.

"We all strike the same night, fight night," I told them. "Dismantle the entire trafficking ring, and *then* I take out Maz," I growled.

"Have I mentioned how sexy vampire Aspen is?" Luka looked over at me with a half-lidded gaze.

Milika watched all of this with her hands covering her mouth in shock. She'd probably been enslaved so long that hearing a mere conversation about an uprising was a shock to her system.

Liv and Ruby looked at each other and nodded. "Well, this king isn't going to want us here tonight anyway, so we might as well head out now, meet up tomorrow night in Idaho."

Luka frowned. "Okay, but let me walk you out. I'm not sure if you'll need an escort."

It was all happening so fast, but I knew that's how it needed to be. If one domino fell too early, it could ruin the entire plan. "You have the names of the leaders of the societies that are involved in this?" I asked Ruby. "The ones who buy the babies and are in on it?"

She nodded. "Yep, all you have to do is follow the money."

"On takedown night," I told her. "I want two teams in each city, a large team to free the women from the magical enclave, and a smaller team to bring me the leaders of each society."

Luka raised an eyebrow. "What are you going to do with them?"

"Truth witch. Magic City Prison," I explained. "But if they get killed in the process ... oh well."

Luka nodded. "Seems fair."

But Maz would meet her death at my hand, that much was sure.

Liv and Ruby stood. I gave them a quick hug as Luka walked them out, leaving just Milika and I.

"Do you have a contract with the ... brothel?" I couldn't bring myself to say "whorehouse."

She nodded. "Lifetime, or until I pay off my debt."

Was that how they got them? "Let me guess, you are born with debt?"

She nodded. "And then it's added to daily for meals and boarding fee."

Bastards.

"Are you hungry?" I picked up a menu for room service and handed it to her.

She glanced at it and her eyes bulged. "Too expensive."

"No. I'm paying. Order whatever you like. Ohhh, truffle fries." I glanced at the menu. "Have you ever had those?" I rattled off a few other items and she shook her head shyly.

Well, if I couldn't eat bacon or chocolate cake anymore, someone was going to!

Picking up the phone, I ordered a smorgasbord of yummy foods and desserts while Milika watched wide-eyed. When I hung up, I reached for the letter Carmen had brought. It was a simple letterhead with an invite for dinner at 7:30 p.m. Which ironically was probably breakfast to the vamps. It had an address I couldn't decipher, but was hoping Milika would help us get there.

We sat in companionable silence while I wondered how much her debt was and if I could convince Luka to pay it. I also kind of wanted to see if he would come to the conclusion on his own about freeing Milika. I mean, we had told her we would get her out of here, but we'd need a solid plan to do that.

When the food came, I watched in fascination and jealousy as Milika ate everything in sight. Chicken fingers, fries, chocolate cake, French onion soup, cobb salad. All my favorites. She kept looking at me nervously while she ate and I realized I was staring.

"Sorry. I was human last week. I miss food," I told her honestly.

She relaxed, grinning. "This is my favorite." She pointed to the chocolate cake.

"Good choice. I don't trust anyone who doesn't like chocolate."

We both erupted into laughter and I felt the lightest I had since getting here.

"What's so funny?" Luka entered with shopping bags on his arm.

"Nothing. What's all that?" I peered over at him.

Luka looked down at our casual clothes. "Dinner with a king. We cannot go in anything less than black tie."

Whatever that means. I stood and walked over to him, reaching into the bag and pulling out a sequined emerald green dress. I grinned. "It's beautiful."

"Like you." Luka winked.

"You are not normal vampires," Milika observed, causing Luka to smile.

"I guess not, huh? Have things always been this way here?" he asked her as I slipped into the bathroom to shower and get ready.

When I was fully dried and slipped into my dress, I peeked my head out and called out to Milika. She was sitting at the edge of the bed talking to Luka, and looked up.

"Can you help me get ready?" I asked. Technically, I could get ready myself, but I wanted to get to know her a little better, and hopefully have her trust me. I knew it must be a shock to have two vampires just barge in like this and say that we were different.

Her face brightened. "Yes I can."

She stepped into the bathroom and I pointed to the curling iron. "Do you know how to?"

She nodded. "My main job at the brothel is sanitation, but I do help the ladies get ready for their ... dates."

The anger rose up inside of me again, but I pushed it down. Those poor women, all born with debt as well I was sure, told they needed to work it off in order to be free. It made me sick.

I changed the subject: "So tell me about your family."

Her cheeks blushed as she grabbed a chunk of my hair and started to curl it. "I lied before so you wouldn't kill me. I have no living family. My nan died a few years back."

I nodded. "I would have lied too."

That brought a goofy grin to her mouth.

"Do you have family?" she asked.

I bobbed my head. "I grew up in an orphanage but recently found my mom and half-sister. They were being held captive in the Idaho breeder farm equivalent to your brothel."

"Oh." Her face darkened. "I can see now why you would take this on."

We continued to talk and get to know each other as she curled my hair and I put on make-up.

An hour later, I was ready for this dinner. The dress fit like a glove, and the green really made my red hair pop.

When I stood and checked myself out in the mirror, Milika smiled. "You look beautiful, madam."

"Thank you." I opened the bathroom door and we stepped out to where Luka was waiting. He undressed me with his eyes, which cause heat to creep up to my cheeks.

Milika consulted her watch. "I should get going. I've got work soon."

Luka and I both shared an alarmed look.

"Go work at the brothel?" he asked.

She nodded. "Thank you for the meal. It was the best I ever had. And for the kindness. It won't be forgotten."

She bowed deeply and moved across the room. I

was about to stop her and run after her when Luka spoke.

"Milika, hang on." Luka stumbled across the room awkwardly. "I don't feel right about letting you go back to work as an indentured servant after you've helped us so much."

She stood there quietly.

"I mean, what if I could … I dunno, buy you? I mean not *really* buy you." He fumbled over his words and I decided to jump in and help the poor guy.

"We'd like to pay your debt and then bring you with us back to Vampire City, where you will be a free troll," I told her.

Her mouth popped open and a small gasp erupted from her. "Pay … my debt? But it's in the thousands. Why … I—"

"Just say the word and I'll handle it with the king tonight," Luka told her. "I gather he's the kind of guy who would like to know that he's done me a favor. I'll owe him and he'll like that."

"He will," she nodded, "That's why you mustn't."

"Milika, we want to help you. Please let us," I pressed her. I could see the scream for help in her eyes, but she didn't want to burden us; it was heartbreaking. I also didn't want to force her to do anything against her will. She'd had enough of that.

"I'll tell you what," Milika offered. "Give me one of those phones to keep in contact with you and I'll remain at my post until you free the women and children. At that time, I will leave with you."

She would help us in our heist? That was risky. From what we saw today in the courtyard, she could be hauled off to jail just for bumping into a vampire!

"Deal," Luka said, and I frowned.

"But if you get caught ... just please be careful," I told her.

She smiled shyly. "You will have a better chance if the women are ready. I want to help, and I'm good at hiding things."

Well, I couldn't argue with that.

Luka handed her his phone and gave her a short tutorial on how it worked and how to turn it off or on, and also to silent, and then she left.

I sat on the edge of the bed. "This has been a crazy day."

Luka knelt before me, running his hands up my ankles and slipping them under the dress to grip my calves. "I have a feeling it's about to get crazier."

I couldn't concentrate on his words with his hands up my dress. I was about to suggest we skip the dinner when he pulled his hands away from my legs and stood. "Come on. We should get going."

With a pout, I took his outstretched fingers and he helped me stand. "Aspen, one thing before we go." His eyes were practically glowing yellow, only a ring of blue on the outer edge. "If we are to mingle with this awful king, you may hear me say or do some things that are ... undesirable, but it's all for show. I assure you."

A stone sank in my gut.

"I understand what must be done," I told him, hoping it wouldn't get too crazy.

He was right, we would have to not only tolerate this man's personality, but also pretend to fit in with a king who held a yearly fight to the death for freedom.

Couldn't wait...

WE STEPPED out of the room and made our way through the hotel and to the outside. There was a driver waiting for us, a male werewolf, leaning up against a bike with a carriage on the back. It reminded me of the tuk-tuks in Thailand.

"Mr. and Mrs. Drake?" The guy waved us over to the sleek black carriage, the steel glint of the slave collar shining at his throat.

I grinned at *Mrs. Drake*. It sounded good. I couldn't wait to marry Luka.

Luka greeted the poor wolf slave, and as we settled into the back seat of the carriage he jumped onto his bike and started pedaling. A light rain fell on the city as he took us down a row of market stalls and then into a wider downtown with bigger buildings. There were lots of people living in these buildings. I counted hundreds of windows and dozens of street carts selling food. The cobblestone pathways made it seem European, but the rest of the vibe was Old World Asian. It was a fascinating place. Troll, vampire, witch, fey and wolf all mixed around together, although the trolls and wolves were clearly of a lower level. Their clothes were dirtier and they walked with their heads low, collars at their throat. It killed me to think that two entire races had been broken here in this city.

The driver rode us past loud bars, pool halls, and other boisterous places to a street that started to thin out from tightly packed buildings to homes with trees. There were houses here, yards, children, families. Well, pureblood fey, vampire and witch families, from what I could see. It was a twenty-minute ride until we reached an even nicer neighborhood, one with a guard gate.

"Here to see King Constantine." The driver bowed his head to a tall sleek vampire, who stepped out of the guard booth.

The guard looked at Luka. "Invitation?"

Luka produced the paper document and the guard looked it over, before peering at me, letting his eyes linger for a moment longer than was polite.

"Is there anything else?" Luka's voice could cut glass.

The guard met my fiancé's eyes and handed the invite back. "Have fun."

The gate opened and then we were driving in. Everything was smaller here, the gates, the roads. I didn't think they had cars here, just the bike carriages.

When we pulled up to the house, I noticed a row of motorcycles and other bike carriages lined up awaiting guests. They were all black. How very vampire.

"Thank you." Luka reached out kindly and squeezed the werewolf's shoulder and he stilled.

"Uh ... you're welcome, sir." The wolf didn't seem used to being thanked.

They're not used to be treated kindly by our people.' Luka's voice in my head was a welcome thing. I had a feeling I would need that to get through this night.

"What's your name?" Luka asked the wolf as we disembarked from the carriage.

The man was about thirty, short but muscular and rough. He had a face full of fine scars, and an unkempt beard. Just behind his eyes was a cagey look that said this man knew how to fight and wouldn't hesitate to defend himself.

"Tink," he mumbled.

Obviously it was a nickname, but from the look of his build and shorter stature, I could see where he got it.

Luka nodded, handing him a twenty dollar bill. "Thank you, Tink."

The guy looked at the money for a moment, blinking stupidly, and I wondered if they didn't use American money here.

"I've already been paid by the king as a part of my service contract," Tink said, and attempted to hand Luka the money back.

I reached out and pushed his hand away. "It's a tip." I winked.

He nodded and stuffed it back in his pocket, looking at Luka and I like we were aliens.

'We're being too nice,' I told Luka.

'Yes, we will need to blend in better inside,' he responded through our bond.

Tink went to stand under the roof overhang, out of the rain with the other drivers. They were all werewolves, I could smell it so strongly now. The gruff bear's giant physique was a dead giveaway too. My gaze fell to the collars at their throats: thin sheets of metal maybe two inches wide.

'Does it keep them from shifting?' I asked Luka.

'*Yes,*' he responded.

They glared at me and I looked down at my feet, running up to the main entrance and out of the rain. They hated us and our kind, and I didn't blame them.

We were two seconds from the giant double doors when they opened. Carmen was waiting to greet us, wearing a tight, red, plunging V-neck dress.

"Mr. and Mrs. Drake, good to see you again." She gave Luka a sugary smile.

"Good evening, Carmen." Luka bowed his head slightly and I was grateful he was raised so proper. I would probably fist bump her if it were left up to me.

We stepped inside and my brain short circuited at what I saw. Luka's hand tightened in my grip as we both took in the scene before us.

'*Shit. It's a feeding party.*' Luka's words were rushed. *I'm going to have to feed on a live woman or they will be suspicious, and it will be rude to decline. You can say you are a new vampire and not yet comfortable with a feeder but—*' He was then cut off by a booming voice.

"Luka Drake!" A man detached himself from a half-naked woman's neck. There were over a dozen lingerie-clad women here, and about the same amount of men in skimpy speedos. *All humans.* For every feeder, there was a vampire dressed in formal attire like us. It looked like a freaking swinger party. I clung to Luka, closely replaying his words.

He'd have to feed from a woman ... my stomach sank.

The man approaching us now, the king I surmised, was the largest vampire I'd ever seen. He must have been seven feet tall, and was extremely muscular, more like a werewolf in stature. But the pale skin, dark eyes, and red-tinged mouth gave away his true nature. His dark hair was slicked back, framing a handsome face, but there was something eerie about him as well, something not right.

Luka extended his hand when he was in reach. "King Constantine. It's a pleasure."

The king gripped Luka's hand, grinning ear to ear. "I've always wanted to meet a Drake. How did you find me?"

Luka paused for a moment, seemingly confused. "We were invited."

"How did you find my city?" the king clarified.

His tone was light but the question was loaded. *Why are you here?* was what he wanted to know.

Luka nodded. "I'm a newly crowned king in

Vampire City over in Idaho. As a part of my inheritance, I was given a map of the other cities."

Not completely the truth, but hopefully the king bought it.

The king's eyes widened. "How many are there?"

Interesting ... he only knew about ours? He must have, since he already knew Luka's name and that I was his fiancée.

"Three more," Luka lied. "New York, Minneapolis, and Austin."

"Fascinating!" The king then drew his eyes to me and his demeaner completely shifted. His posture straightened and eyes went half-lidded as he reached for my hand.

I plastered a smile on my face. "Hello, sir. I'm Aspen, Luka's fiancée."

He bent slowly and kissed the top of my hand lightly.

"Ah, young love, before the cheating and betrayal ruins your marriage," he said dryly, and then burst into unhinged laughter.

Luka matched his laughter and so I followed, trying to pretend that was a totally normal thing to say when meeting someone for the first time.

The dude seemed a bit deranged, so I was just going to have to read the room and play along.

"Is it true you fight to the death for your crowns?" the king suddenly asked Luka.

My hubby-to-be lifted his shirt and showed the king his abs. They were littered with scars and tattoos. "It's true."

The king clapped in enjoyment. "I love it!"

Luka tucked his shirt back in, and smiled at the king. The king was lapping it up, grinning ear to ear.

'Weirdo,' I sent to Luka, but he didn't respond.

"Monica!" the king snapped, and a brunette feeder wearing a red skimpy lingerie number pulled herself away from the wall she'd been leaning on.

The king leaned into Luka and lowered his voice. "She tastes like honey. She's my favorite, but I want you to enjoy her."

Mother fricker. I squeezed Luka's hand so hard he cleared his throat.

The king noticed and looked at me skeptically.

"She's newly changed. Days old actually," Luka told him.

Thank God he didn't mention my fragile feelings or I would have throat punched him.

The king nodded his head in understanding. "I see. A delicate time. You may take your pick of the men, my dear. Any one of them would be lucky to have you." He gestured to the male models standing in speedos against the wall, and my stomach growled.

The king clapped his hands in excitement. "Did you hear that? She's hungry!"

Now it was Luka's turn to squeeze my hand.

'You don't have to,' he told me. *'I'll tell the king you aren't ready.'*

I looked at him. *'We have to play the part.'* I glared at Monica as she approached my man. *'Touch anything on her body but her wrist and I'll remove your balls and shove them down your throat.'*

'Yes, ma'am,' Luka responded.

I turned, leaving Luka to be with Monica, and walked over to the first guy I could find.

'You like blonds? Interesting,' Luka commented.

'Oh hush, he's the first one I could grab.' I smiled at the dude.

'Grab nothing. Wrist only,' he parroted my words and I grinned wider.

"Hungry, My Lady?" the guy asked me, and my stomach tightened into knots. Drink from a freaking human? Gross.

I mean, I *was* hungry, but it was just so against everything I believed. This was by far the worst part of being a vampire.

"Does Mrs. Drake not find my feeders to her

liking?" the king called over my shoulder and I froze, plastering a fake smile on my face.

"Oh, he'll do fine." I looked over my shoulder and winked at the king, who grinned mischievously at me.

Double gross.

Grasping the dude's wrist, I pulled him away with me into one of the feeder rooms that I'd seen Luka go into.

When I stepped inside, I was assaulted with the smell of fresh blood and four different couples feeding. Luka was in the corner, Monica's wrist to his mouth. As he watched me enter, his eyes sharpened.

Did Monica just moan? *Oh hell no.*

'I'm going to kill her,' I spat at Luka. *'After this, you're drinking bottled blood for the rest of your life!'*

'Yes, dear,' he retorted, and was that a smile creeping up the edge of his lips?

Let's freaking get this over with.

'Pretend you're biting into an apple, and then tip the apple back and drink it's juice,' Luka coached me. *'It won't hurt him.'*

I knew that, I'd been fed from more times than I could count. In fact, I was pretty sure it was going to feel good for the guy, which gave me the creeps.

Pulling the guy's wrist to my mouth, I looked at

him, wondering if I should expressly ask permission or something. But the eagerness in his eyes was permission alone.

Gross, gross, gross, I thought as I pulled his wrist to my lips, focusing on the pulse I could hear and now *feel* against my tongue. My teeth lengthened and I closed my eyes, doing as Luka had suggested and envisioning an apple. The moment my teeth pierced his flesh, he moaned throatily and I winced.

'Motherfucker, I want to rip his head off,' Luka growled from across the room.

An explosion of flavor burst across my tongue more vibrant and potent than the bottled blood. I drank it greedily, ignoring Luka's voice in my head. The hunger had taken over me and I was too enthralled in this flavor bomb to care that my soon-to-be husband was jealous. My eyes were still closed when the feeder's free hand came up around my waist and stroked my hip.

"Touch her and die." Luka's voice sounded inches from me. My eyes snapped open and Luka was hovering over the feeder's back with a red-tinged mouth and glowing eyes. The feeder dropped his hand from my hip, looked at Luka and paled.

Taking one last sip, I gulped down the rest of my meal and lowered his wrist. The feeder slipped away, running for the door as fast as he could, and Luka stepped closer to me, the veins in his neck bulging.

'We're never doing that again,' he stated.

I grinned, enjoying his jealousy a tiny bit. *'Sounds like a plan.'*

We exited the room hand in hand and I was wondering when it would be polite to leave and go back to the hotel, when I heard a commotion outside.

"Gather round! The fights are beginning," Carmen called out to the party, and everyone rushed forward to press outside.

'Fights?' My stomach dropped.

'King Constantine clearly likes bloodshed,' Luka answered.

We were swept outside with the crowd, and my gaze brushed over the lush, well-manicured gardens. There was an open grassy area at least an acre wide that had been set up to host the party. White tealights lined the outer edge of the garden, and there were hundreds of white folding chairs out on the lawn. They all surrounded a square mat where two werewolves in human form stood.

My stomach sank when I realized they were going to make the wolves fight for their entertainment.

The king waved us over and Luka plastered on a fake smile, linking his arm into mine.

I was surprised to see witches and fey standing around as well. They were all coming into a side gate that looked to be guarded.

"My special guests get the front row seats!" The king tapped two high-backed chairs next to his.

Great.

Striding forward, the crowd parted and we sat next to the king, with Luka sitting closest to him. The gathered crowd started to take their seats as well. Fey, witch, and vampire mixed about, seeming to chat among each other and get along well. That was something positive here at least, in the fact that they didn't segregate the supernaturals like we did.

Carmen walked over to the wolves on the fighting mat and checked something on their collars. Probably making sure they were still secure.

'Those hurt,' Luka growled in my mind, and I looked over at him.

'What? The collars?'

'I wore one for years in prison and they fucking hurt.' He gave King Constantine a side glare and my heart fell. We never talked much about his time in prison.

'I'm sorry. Just play it cool. We can't save everyone.

Focus on the goal.' I reached out and squeezed his thigh.

He nodded once, swallowing hard.

"Place your bets!" Carmen yelled into a PA system, and the feeders in lingerie made their way down the aisles collecting money and noting names. When they got to Luka, he pulled a wad of cash out of his pocket and pointed to the small wolf. I realized then that it was our driver, Tink.

The woman raised her eyebrow. "You sure about that?"

"Never underestimate an underdog," Luka told her, and handed her the money. She shrugged and left.

The king laughed, patting Luka on the back. "Is it true you were in prison for many years?"

Luka and I both bristled at the same time and the king noticed.

He gave Luka a knowing side look. "Wondering how I know all of these things?"

Luka was very still, as if he might pounce at any moment.

The king grinned, seemingly enjoying my man's discomfort. "I have a well-traveled friend. She trades information with me as a part of our business arrangement."

For some reason, Maz popped into my mind. She couldn't be here though, right? She wasn't that well connected ... or was she? Perhaps he meant the leader of the Los Angeles Vampire Hunter Society. Either way, they knew things about Luka and our world and we knew nothing about them, which was uncomfortable.

"I shall need a similar friend, then," Luka told him. "So that I can find out about you."

It was a veiled threat, and the king noticed. I could tell by the tic in his jaw. "Well, isn't that why you're here?"

"Indeed." Luka smiled, but it didn't reach his eyes.

A bell dinged, breaking the tension, and our attention was brought to the fight.

'I don't trust him,' I said suddenly as the werewolves started to go at it. They punched each other wildly and without restraint.

'I haven't trusted him from the second we walked in. Too chatty. Too gleeful. He's hiding something, and he knows too much.'

My stomach soured. I had totally trusted him in the beginning of the night. Some good sense of character I was!

'What's the plan?' I straightened, suddenly alert and ready for an ambush.

Luka watched the fight as the men proceeded to tear into each other. Ugh, I'd seen enough of these fights during Luka's trial to last me a lifetime. I stayed quiet, focusing on the garden beyond the fight as the match raged on and the crowd cheered. Luka screamed in excitement and the king growled, which pulled my attention back to the mat. Our driver, Tink, the smaller man that Luka had bet on, had the throat of the larger man in his hands. The bigger dude was turning purple.

"Call it," the king told Carmen.

Carmen rang the bell and the smaller wolf released his hold on the larger one.

Interesting. The king didn't let them kill each other? Maybe he wanted to save his big wolf for another day. The crowd looked sullen, most of them probably betting on the larger wolf, but a few had wide grins, including Luka.

The king appraised my fiancé. "You made a good call."

"Underdogs have more fighting spirit," Luka told him.

The king nodded as the lingerie-clad human walked over and handed Luka a fat stack of cash, at least quadruple what he'd given her initially.

"You know, I wonder who would win in a fight between you and I," the king said suddenly.

I stiffened as Luka casually handed me his stack of cash and looked over at the king.

"I thought I was here as your guest," Luka told him.

The king shrugged. "You are. But I can't *really* trust someone until I know how strong they are. What if you are here to take over my kingdom?"

Crap, this was derailing fast.

"I assure you, I'm not," Luka deadpanned.

The king nodded. "I would respect you more if you would honor me with a fight."

'What the hell is he doing?' I asked Luka.

'This is the way he works,' Luka responded.

"If you and your people want a show, let's give them one." Luka started to unbutton his dress shirt and the king grinned, clapping Luka on the shoulder.

"Good man. An honest man!" he roared, and then stood.

'He's unhinged,' I said.

'He reminds me of the mad king. I wonder how old he is,' Luka observed.

'Let's leave right now,' I begged. *'You don't have to fight him.'*

'Yes I do. It will win us his trust so when we come back and steal the women and children, he won't know what hit him.'

Frick.

'Luka, what if you get hurt? He's huge.'

Luka pulled off his shirt, highlighting his cut physique, and glared at me. Oops, wrong thing to say. I'd seen him fight. He was a maniac. I should have been more supportive.

'I'll have to let him win. I can't embarrass him in front of his people, but I'll hurt him enough to gain his respect.'

Ugh, was this seriously happening right now?

Carmen tapped the mic and the supernaturals present quieted.

"Our king has a special guest, and they have agreed to entertain us!" she bellowed into the mic. The people present cheered and clapped. It was a much less rowdy crowd than it was for Luka's trials, but the fact that this was normal behavior baffled me.

"Not a fight to the death of course, but just to see who will tap out first," she purred.

Well, that was obviously going to be Luka, whether he was winning or not. He was right in that he couldn't embarrass the king in front of his people.

"Place your bets!" Carmen cried out.

Great.

'Bet against me. He'll like that,' Luka told me.

What?

This was so stupid!

The king watched in delight as money started to exchange hands. From the whispers I could hear, nearly everyone was betting on him. I'm sure his ego loved that.

"My Lady?" the lingerie-clad woman asked.

I locked eyes with the king, who was watching me. "My bet is on King Constantine."

Luka frowned, faking obviously, and the king grinned.

Carmen brought the mic back to her lips. "Our king has survived many battles, conquered many lands, and even fought dragons. Let's see how he fares with Luka Drake!"

The crowd went wild, and I swallowed hard at the mention of him fighting dragons. I also noticed they weren't referring to Luka as a king himself.

Interesting. This entire trip had not been what I expected, but I suppose it could be worse.

'Dragons?' I balked.

'He must be very, very old,' Luka surmised. *'They used to roam our world freely.'*

The king removed his shirt as well, and my eyes

trailed down the angry puckered scar over his heart. There was a story there, I was sure.

'No weapons?' I glanced around the space.

'He doesn't seem the type. I prefer bareknuckle fighting anyway. Reminds me of prison.'

I shouldn't be turned on by that, but I was. Luka met my gaze and winked, then the king strode forward and reached out to shake Luka's hand. My hubby-to-be grasped the king's hand and shook it, but his body was coiled like a snake about to strike.

"Let's do this!" Carmen called out, and the bell dinged.

All I could think of was what a horrible idea it had been to come here.

No sooner had the chime of the bell rang throughout the garden did the king charge forward and tackle Luka like a football player. The breath whooshed out of my man and he was knocked backward. The king tried to crawl on top of him and pin him down, but Luka pulled his legs back and then kicked out. His feet connected with the king's chest and he went flying, causing the crowd to gasp. King Constantine landed gracefully on his feet, the grass bunching up behind his heels as he skidded backward.

Luka kicked up into a standing position, facing the king, and both of the men grinned.

It was game on. They ran at each other terrifyingly fast. With a loud crack they bashed into each other and started throwing punches.

The thuds of fists smacking flesh filled the yard. I winced as blood flew left and right. Luka dodged a few, but the king was getting some really good hits on his face.

Don't hurt his beautiful face!

With a burst of energy, Luka struggled out of the king's hold and zoomed to the side. His cheek was bloodied and bruised and the crowd cheered wildly.

"Yes!" the king shouted at the sky like a maniac, laughing as blood dripped from his nose.

'He's losing it. He'll be a mad king within a year,' Luka stated.

Luka charged forward and the king kicked out, landing a foot squarely on Luka's chest. I heard the bones in Luka's ribs crack from here as my man went flying across the garden.

Bastard!

I stood, rushing forward without thinking, but a hand grasped my wrist and yanked me back before I could make it into the ring.

I looked behind me with a glare. It was Tink. He was bloodied yet healing. He shook his head slightly and then removed his hand from my wrist.

I sucked in a few breaths, trying to calm myself.

That bastard just broke Luka's ribs, but Tink was right. I couldn't intervene.

The king let loose another maniacal laugh, then Luka charged out of nowhere, a blur as he burst from the garden hedge and tackled the king to the ground.

Breathing a little easier, I stepped back into the shadows to stand beside the werewolf fighters, and a mix of fey and witch.

If it looked like Luka was losing, I was going to stop this. I no longer trusted this crazy king to end the fight before someone got killed.

Luka was able to pin the king beneath his arms and rain blow after blow onto his face and chest while the king cackled maniacally and did little to fight back.

'He wants to die?' I observed.

'He likes pain. I've been there,' Luka answered, and chills ran up my arms.

Luka slowed his punches, probably realizing he could actually kill him at this point, or that it was getting to be more than just a friendly fight, and the king burst upward, bucking Luka off.

Luka fell to the side, but also forward in an awkward position and slammed his face onto the mat. Falling onto his stomach, the king stood over him, grinding a boot into his back. Luka tried to move but the king was too strong, too big, and when he leaned down and reached his hands around my future husband's throat, my stomach dropped.

"You win!" Luka cried out, but the king didn't move.

The crowd went wild, and Carmen did nothing to call off the fight. Panic seized me as the king started to twist Luka's neck.

I ran toward Carmen with every ounce of vampire speed I had and chucked her out of the way with a bump of my hip. Reaching out, I yanked the cord on the bell and it chimed. The king looked up, noticing it was me who had rung the bell, and grinned.

He released Luka and the crowd went wild.

'He was testing you to see what you would do,' Luka told me.

I glared at the king. *'Well, I was about to break a leg off this chair and ram it into his heart.'*

The king reached out and offered Luka his hand, pulling him up to his feet, and then into a hug. He rapped Luka two times on the back and whispered something in his ear. The crowd was roaring too loudly for me to hear it, but when he pulled away Luka wore a tight smile.

'What did he say?' I asked.

'He said he knew I went easy on him, and next time I

should kill him. He's gone mad.' Luka met my gaze and I swallowed hard.

Dealing with a mad king was not on the agenda for this trip.

'Let's go home,' I told him. He was bleeding and limping. They both were. Idiots.

"Have a drink with me!" The king called Luka over to a bar and they veered that way.

Ugh, great. We were stuck here for another hour at least, and God knows what would happen in that time.

'Wait, can we drink alcohol?'

Luka followed the king but replied to me. *'Yep. Can get pretty piss drunk too, but it wears off quickly.'*

Interesting. I wasn't a big fan of drinking, but good to know I could if I wanted to.

'But why don't you pee it out?' I asked.

Luka looked back at me, slightly annoyed. *'I don't know, ask a scientist. Why are you obsessed with peeing?'*

I shrugged. *'I used to do it like ten times a day. I kinda miss it.'*

He chuckled, shaking his head, and met the king at the bar.

The woman came over to me with my winnings, which were obscenely large, probably into the thousands. I took the two stacks of money and scanned the garden for our driver, Tink. He'd helped me keep my cool when I'd almost attacked the king, and I wanted to reward him.

He was dabbing his split lip, talking with another werewolf in the corner. When I approached, he bowed his head deeply. "My apologies for before, madam, I should not have touched you—"

"I wanted to thank you for your help," I told him, and handed him the wad of cash. We didn't need it, and I didn't want to carry it around this party all night.

He eyes landed on the stack in my hand and widened to saucers. "Umm, you're welcome, but—"

I shoved the money forward and it hit his chest. "Take it. That's an *order.*"

A slow grin played out on his face and he nodded, grabbing the money and slipping it into his pocket. "Yes, ma'am."

I couldn't help but stare at the collar on his neck and the scars around the edges of it. I remembered what Luka said about them hurting, and stories I knew about Demi struggling with hers as well.

Leaning forward, I lowered my voice so that it was barely audible. "Fey blades cut off the collars," I whispered, the background noise of the crowd behind me drowning out my voice to any lurkers.

His eyebrows hit his hairline, and he shared a look with his friend, who'd stopped smoking his cigarette mid puff.

"Who are you?" he asked.

"Are you sure?" the friend said, tossing the lit half smoke to the ground and snuffing it out with his boot.

I nodded once and then walked away. I'd already lingered too long. I didn't want anyone at the party thinking I favored werewolves when it was not seen as an acceptable thing for vampires to do. Especially considering the king killed his own wife over fraternizing with a wolf. This whole city was so different to ours and I needed to toe the line. Yet, if those boys wanted to break free, at least now they knew it was possible with a fey blade. Something Demi had told me.

By the time I made it to the bar, Luka was pounding a shot with the king. Both were still shirtless, crusted blood and healing wounds dotting their bodies.

Luka gave me a cautious look as I approached. The king let his eyes run up and down my body slowly, his first deliberate show of attraction toward me. "Tell me, Aspen, if I had killed him, what would you have done?"

I paused for a moment, unsure how to play my hand before I decided the lunatic would probably enjoy the truth. Stepping forward, I plastered a sugary smile on my face and draped my arms around Luka's shoulders. "Oh, I would have ripped your head clean off and shoved it up your ass. Carmen's too, for not stopping the fight."

There was a pause and Luka flinched next to me, before the king burst into maniacal laughter. "Ruthless. I *love* her. Please tell me she has a sister," he asked Luka.

Luka relaxed a little. "She does not."

"A best friend?" The king raised one eyebrow.

An idea formed in my mind. "I do. She's human actually, one of Luka's feeders. I'd be happy to introduce you to her if we are invited back?"

The king's eyes practically heated with desire. "Why don't you come back next weekend? I'm having my annual Freedom Fight."

Luka played dumb. "What's that?"

"All the slaves beat each other senseless. The last one standing gets to go free," the king bragged.

Luka grinned, although I knew he was just playing the part, and the conversation made him as sick as it made me. "Sounds like good entertainment. I'd like to see that."

The king regarded Luka for a moment. "You should come, as my guest. It's next week. How long are you staying?"

"Just the night I'm afraid. I have to get back to my people. But I would love to attend the fight. Maybe I could bring some of my men who would enjoy it as well?"

The king paused, eyeing Luka.

"And maybe you could come visit our lands?" I interjected, so it didn't sound suspicious. "Our wedding is in a month."

The king's eyes grew wide. "I've wanted to see another magic city since I was a young vampire. I would love to."

Luka grinned. "Then it's settled! I think you will enjoy the open fields of Vampire City. We can have a gala in *your* honor."

The king grinned. "Alright, then. Next week, bring this feeder friend and twelve of your men. I will show you a good time."

Luka reached out and shook his hand. "It's a plan."

The king hugged him then, messing up Luka's hair like he was a teenage younger brother. "You earned my trust. Now don't break it."

Luka gave a nervous laugh and I forced myself to

yawn. "Babe, I'm not used to the time change. Can you take me back to the hotel? I'm exhausted."

Luka nodded, looking at the king. "I'm afraid I must get my bride-to-be to bed."

The king grasped Luka's shoulder. "We are well met, Luka Drake." And then reached out to me and grasped my hand lightly. He bent down and kissed it.

"Thank you for having us." I kept it short and sweet, because saying it was a lovely evening would have been too much of a stretch for me.

"The pleasure was all mine." His eyes glittered as they raked over my body once more.

Creeper.

We stepped away from him and I made eye contact with our driver, tipping my head toward the side gate. He pushed off the wall and headed toward us.

'I saw the fat tip you gave him.' Luka grasped my hand and led me out the gate.

'Do you mind?' I chewed my lip. *'I feel bad for the wolves.'*

Luka grinned, pulling my fingers up to his lips and kissing the knuckles. *'I don't mind at all. In fact, I was thinking of doing the same.'*

As we drove away from the king's house, a million thoughts ran through my mind. But the single most prominent was how in the hell were we going to get these girls out of a building we hadn't even seen, while Luka and I were guests of honor at a fight packed with supernaturals?

The only solution might involve whoring my best friend out as a feeder, and that made me sick.

IN CASE ANYONE WAS WATCHING, we stayed at the hotel another six hours to make it seem like we were resting, then we hightailed it out of there. I texted Milika and told her we were invited for fight night and to be ready to flee then. She took forever to respond, and her text was riddled with typos, but she said she would be ready, and would help in any way she could. I asked her for a map of the city, pointing out where the breeding house was, and she said she would get back to me.

We had less than a week to plan a takeover of a foreign magical place, and it was nerve racking. The second we got home, Luka called a meeting with Demi and the others for the very next day when they would all be back from their missions of scouting out the other cities. I laid low with my mom and

Maple doing wedding stuff, and tried not to stress about the impending takeover of Night City.

"I was thinking a light blush cream for your bridesmaids' dresses." My mom showed me a few styles in a catalogue.

"Ohh yeah, those are pretty!" Sage, Maple, and Demi had all agreed to be my bridesmaids, with Liv being my maid of honor.

There was a knock at the door and I stood. "I'll get it."

Mom and Maple had really taken to this plan-my-wedding thing, and I liked it because all I had to do was point to stuff I adored and they made it happen. This knock on the door was probably a delivery of wedding stuff.

Pulling open the door, I greeted the delivery person in a khaki uniform, who handed me a small white box. "Aspen Rose?" he asked.

I nodded, taking the box from him. "Thanks," I said, and he dipped his head once before turning to jog back to his truck.

Shutting the door, I started to rip open the package. "Let me guess, it's my veil?" I asked my mom.

She smiled. "Could be, but looks too small. Maybe it's your—"

I yelped in pain, cutting her off as I'd reached

into the box and grasped a cold hard stone. A shock ran up my arm and into my chest, squeezing my heart.

"Aspen!" my mom yelled.

I staggered backward, dropping the box and shaking my arm out as if it would make the pain lessen.

When the box hit the ground, a light blue crystal rolled out.

"Don't touch it," I barked at my mother, who bent to pick it up. I knew this feeling somehow.

I'd just been spelled.

Using my foot, I dug through the rest of the box's contents until I found what I was looking for.

A card.

Kicking the card open, I knelt down and read:

ASPEN, *for the lovely bride to be. Now you can't ever kill me.*

-Maz

MY MOM LOOKED at me with concern. "A spell?"

Even she knew. Frick, this was bad, this was really bad.

I chewed my lip, shaking my arm again. The pain was lessening; my chest felt lighter. But I couldn't escape the feeling that something permanent had just been done to me.

"Call Luka." I gulped.

My mom nodded and ran to the kitchen, where her phone was. About ten minutes later Luka charged into the room with Demi and a young woman my age. A witch, my nose told me. She had dark hair and was holding a bundle of smoking sage. She fanned it toward me and it burst into flames.

"Oh dear," the witch said.

Crap. That sounded bad.

"What is it?" Luka looked panicked at the letter and crystal on the floor.

The witch bent and peered at the card. "She's been cursed. A life curse. If she tries to harm the sender, she will be harmed instead."

My stomach dropped. "No!"

Maz was mine to kill. I *had* to.

"But she'll be okay if she doesn't touch Maz?" Luka strode over to me and pulled me into his arms.

The witch nodded. "She will."

Luka smooshed me against his chest, his arms wrapping around me.

Demi hugged the witch. "Thank you, Raven."

I sank into Luka's embrace and tried not to freak out. If I laid a finger on Maz, it would harm me? I wondered what would happen if she tried to bait me into attacking her?

Luka must have been thinking the same thing, because he looked over at Raven as Demi moved to walk her out. "How do we get the curse off of her?"

Raven frowned at me. "Someone else needs to kill the sender."

Luka went rigid beside me, and I looked up into his eyes.

'Remember when I told you I couldn't kill Morgana because of the Sire-Fledgling Pact? You said you would kill her for me...'

I nodded, knowing where this was going. How could I ever forget that steamy moment in the shower?

'I will kill Maz for you. Mark my words, my love.'

I nodded, feeling the rightness of that. I would kill Morgana for him, and he would kill Maz for me.

"Thank you," I told the witch, and she gave me a smile before stepping outside with Demi.

A few moments later, Demi returned and cleaned up the crystal and card, throwing it into the trash. "Is now a bad time for the meeting? Sawyer and the others just got in and we have so much to tell you both." She looked at me curled in Luka's arms and I broke free, shaking myself.

"No, it's fine. I need a distraction. Besides, the curse is done. There's nothing I can do about it."

She bobbed her chin up and down. "Alright, then, let's do it."

I reassured my mom that I was fine about fifty times, and then Luka and I walked with Demi over to the main meeting hall in the castle. Luka had arranged some light catering for those in our group who still required food, and we sat around a large table, chatting.

"You go first," Demi told us as she tucked into a huge roast beef sandwich.

Luka and I exchanged a look. Where did we even begin with our story of Night City?

"So, they are led by a vampire who is going mad," I started off.

"But we made an ally and left her with my phone," Luka added, and then we launched into the whole story and everything we did and saw.

Sawyer's mouth opened when Luka told him about the fighting.

"He fought you?" Sawyer asked.

"It was weird. It wasn't a real fight. He wanted to show off and test me and Aspen," Luka told him.

Sawyer whistled low. "Sounds tough, but glad you got invited back in a week. I'll join you."

Luka and I froze. We hadn't told him yet that the werewolves were basically slaves there, and Demi obviously hadn't said anything to him either.

"The werewolves aren't exactly friends of the vampires there," Luka hedged.

"Just tell him," Demi said, her jaw tightening.

Sawyer frowned. "Tell me what?"

We were surrounded by Ruby, Vasquez, Sage, Walsh, Liv, Rab, and Marmal, and it felt like a very personal and serious thing to tell someone their entire race was enslaved.

Luka stayed silent, unable to do it, so I was the one. "The werewolves and trolls in Night City are slaves. They all wear shock collars."

Sawyer's entire body flinched. He squeezed his sandwich so hard it fell in half. Demi, Walsh, Sage, they all wore similar expressions. Marmal too.

"But…" I tried to lighten the mood. "I told them that fey blades remove the collars."

Demi nodded. "Maybe some of them can spread the word and they can break free. They could come here."

Sawyer looked at his wife, bobbing his head in agreement. "When you go back, spread the word to the wolves that if any want to break free and join our pack, they are welcome. Tell them how to get here."

Relief spread through me. I would love to tell them that. "I'll do that."

"Tell us about your visit," Luka asked Sawyer.

"NOLA Magic City is exactly like here. Once we told the local alpha about the breeding program, he agreed to take it down and send us proof it was done. He'll do it on whatever night we want so that we can coordinate."

Sawyer's words brought such relief, I nearly collapsed into the chair.

I looked at Ruby. "And what about Austin?"

She and Liv traded a look, then Ruby spoke: "There are barely any purebloods in Austin's magic city. They're really predominantly Ithaki. Everyone else is mixed with varying powers. The king and queen are both Ithaki, and they despise pure bloods. They offered to hunt down the fey encampment and free the women before wiping out the Munai or whoever is in charge."

Okay, checkmark on that city! This was amazing news.

"Walsh?" Luka looked to one of his best friends.

"Chicago was similar to Idaho. Local alpha says

he will take care of it, and he sends his thanks on letting him know about the issue."

"Same with ours," Vasquez added. "We went to the vampire king and he agreed that if you tell him the day, they will take it all down. They are already at war with the fey. He seemed excited to have a reason to invade their territory."

Ruby yipped in excitement, and I couldn't help but feel the same as well.

"So Los Angeles is really our only problem," I mused.

"And our home turf," Sawyer commented. "In order to really stop this, we need to stop people from buying the babies in the first place."

"We need to take out Maz. She's the mastermind," I told them.

Everything led back to Maz and the leaders of the societies that she had brainwashed. I hadn't yet told everyone that I was now cursed and wouldn't be able to harm her. But it needed to be done or they would just regroup.

"If we kill Maz first, the other cities might spook and shut down or go into hiding," Ruby mused.

I nodded. "She'll have to be last. As well as the other society leaders. And we'll need to get proof out to all the hunters what she was doing. Then they can rebuild the society from the ground up."

Ruby nodded. "Aspen, once you guys take out Los Angeles, and the other cities free their breeders, you could bait Maz and finish her off."

Liv nodded. "Ruby and I could lead small hunter teams to the society houses in each city and take out their corrupt leader. In one night we end this whole thing."

Luka looked at me and I squirmed under his gaze. "I won't be taking out Maz."

Ruby's head reeled back in shock. "Oh, okay. I thought you wanted to? I can go after her with my team, but I figured since you're a vampire now—"

"No, you're right and I *do* want to," I told Ruby. "But she cursed me a few hours ago and now I can't harm her or that harm will come back onto me."

The entire table fell silent.

Luka squeezed my hand and then looked at Ruby. "But you're right in that it needs to be a vampire that takes her out. Maz is a Munai and she's strong. I will kill her for Aspen."

Kill for me? Sounded crazy, but it was romantic.

Ruby looked relieved. "Well, that's settled, then. When is the fight?"

"Saturday night," Luka confirmed.

Everyone around the table nodded. We had five days to bring down an entire empire.

"We'll need more hunters," Ruby said. "I can split up my guys, but—"

The door of the meeting room opened and Luka's new assistant poked his head in. "Umm we have an issue at the gates," he said.

Luka stood. "What issue?"

His assistant pointed at Ruby. "More hunters like her. They say they're here to see Aspen."

Shock filtered through me. More hunters ... here to see *me*?

"House of Rose!" Liv sprang up, "They must have gotten the email and believed us!"

Excitement thrummed through me and I lurched forward, but Luka's hand came out to block me. "Or it's a trap."

My excitement deflated like a popped balloon. "They wouldn't..." I wasn't sure though. I was a vampire now and they had seen that. I burned their freaking house down! They might not trust me.

"They could be here to get the inside scoop for Maz," Ruby agreed. "It took over a week for me to convince my team of the truth. Brainwashing takes time to unravel."

House of Rose. My friends. My fellow hunters. Were they here to spy on me?

"But if they *are* in need, we can't turn them away…" I looked to Luka, hoping he'd come up with something brilliant.

He squirmed under my gaze, reaching up to rub the back of his head.

"We can take them." Sawyer stood and Demi nodded.

"They won't be able to hear about the plan or see what's going on this week in Werewolf City," Demi added.

Relief rushed over me. "Thank you!"

I sidestepped Luka and walked over to Liv. "Let's go greet them, drop them off at Werewolf City, and just say we have no room for them here."

She nodded. "Good plan."

"I'll come too," Ruby added.

"Be safe!" Luka called out after me as I was already halfway out the door.

'Meet up with you later.' I blew an air kiss to Luka and he gave me a lopsided grin.

'Those shorts are so short they look like underwear,' he scolded me.

'Oh you love it,' I told him, swaying my hips as I crossed the room.

'I'd like them a lot better on the floor of our bedroom,' he replied through our bond.

My face heated, which was saying a lot for a vampire, and then we stepped out of the room and made our way to the city gates.

WE GREETED the House of Rose hunters. Over thirty of them. They seemed weary and down but excited to see us. When we told them they couldn't stay in Vampire City and would have to go to Werewolf City, a few of them bailed and said they were leaving. The others pushed the issue, asking why they couldn't stay with us, and I wondered if Luka was right and they were sent as spies. Eventually they relented and agreed to stay in Werewolf City while we made more permanent accommodations for them.

We followed them over to Werewolf City in Demi's car, and when we stepped out at Sterling Hill Academy, the House of Rose hunters gathered round, full of questions. They clung to their backpacks, looking around the academy as if expecting an attack at any moment.

Holly seemed to be the leader of the group. She

barely let Demi get in a word of greeting before she rattled off her questions: "How did you get those papers you emailed and how long did Sterling know about it?" Holly glared at me.

"You expect us to believe Maz is some … evil cult leader and we aren't even human?" Anthony asked.

I never liked Holly. She was two years older than me and a know-it-all.

I shrugged. "Maz is more than that. She's a Munai. A really dark fey."

All thirty pairs of eyes bulged. I knew I would get nowhere with them. They would have to see it firsthand.

"It was Sterling's handwriting!" Valerie stated. "I compared it to his Christmas card last year. It's all true."

They started to argue between themselves and rattle off more questions, then Liv cleared her throat beside me. "Aspen found her mom!" she screamed boldly, and the chatter died down as every mouth dropped open.

"What?" Holly glared at Liv like she had just said something unforgivable.

Liv nodded. "Some of your moms might still be alive. Here in Werewolf City or in Vampire City. We split the task of taking the refugees that we freed from the breeder camp."

The hunters started to squirm, as if this idea hadn't crossed their minds yet. The idea that their own mothers might still be alive...

"That's right, so if you would stop accusing us of lying, you can meet my mom and start to look for your own," I snapped, a little annoyed at the accusations flying around. I knew hearing the truth was rough. I'd had to go through my own little mini breakdown. But I had no reason to make this stuff up.

"I'm here," my mom's voice called from behind me, and I stiffened.

Every single gaze locked on to my mom, and then danced from her to me. Other than my dyed red hair, it was obvious we were related. I smiled at Sage, who stood just behind my mother. She'd foreseen this proof and had brought her here.

A younger hunter whose name I couldn't remember stumbled forward. "Do you know my mom?" Her bottom lip quivered.

My mom's eyes glistened with tears. "What's your name, honey? They let us name you. It's the only thing we can remember you by."

"Harlow," she croaked.

Yes, Harlow. She was a junior hunter, barely seventeen. Sterling trained her.

A light dawned upon my mother's face. "Harlow and Holly are Althea's girls. She's in Vampire City right now."

Holly went stiff as a board, looking at Harlow with a keen eye. They both had the same mousy brown hair and hazel eyes. *Holy crap.*

"Sisters?" Holly asked my mom.

"Are you Holly? How old are you?" my mother asked. "We know all of our children's birthdates and names. I can get you all sorted. Don't worry."

A male hunter stepped forward. "What about me? I'm Noah."

"I'm Riv." Another pushed to the front.

A female sidestepped Noah to get closer to my mom. "Penelope? Born in August? Do you know my mother?"

My heart shattered in that moment. Whatever biases they had come in with were gone. They all just wanted to find their birth mother, to have a family outside of the one Maz had created from lies.

"Mom, you okay?" I asked, because she looked slightly overwhelmed with emotion.

Reaching out, she grasped my hand and

squeezed. "I've got this. It's my way to help, and I'm honored to do so."

My throat clenched with emotion. When she told me she wanted to help us free the breeders, I envisioned her giving us intel that would help us attack the encampment, but this ... this was so much more important. I nodded, not trusting myself to speak.

"Penelope, you are Joyce's daughter. She died last winter I'm afraid." My mom's tone was somber and Penelope's head dipped low. "But your younger sister is here, in Werewolf City," my mom added, and Penelope looked up with a bright smile. "She was a breeder."

My mom then looked to the next hunter. "Riv, your mother, Laura, is here too. One of my oldest friends," my mom said, and he broke into a full-on grin, a single tear slipping down his cheek.

Demi suddenly appeared next to me, pulling me away from the crowd. I looked up at her and could tell immediately by the look on her face that it was serious.

"Oh God, what's wrong?" I asked.

Demi stepped away so that we wouldn't be overheard, and then chewed on her bottom lip. "Would a good friend tell you something you've been wanting to know even if it might derail this cushy little family reunion?" she asked.

I frowned. "Yes?" I was confused at what she was talking about.

Demi swallowed hard, and then a light bulb went off in my head.

"Morgana," I growled.

Demi grinned. "I got the bitch's location. She's a day's journey away. Pearl can fly us in, you take care of her, and we will be back by tonight. What do you say?"

I grinned. Demi was the best.

"Oh *hell* yeah," I told her.

Morgana not only tried to kill me, she hurt Luka, and his mom. I was going to kill her slowly and enjoy every second of it.

I hesitated. "I should tell Luka…"

Demi nodded. "I need to tell Sawyer too. Best to tell them *after* we leave."

I snort-chuckled, and then called Liv over so we could all slip away to Paladin Village.

Morgana was going down.

'TELL DEMI *you can never hang out with her again,*' Luka roared as I clung to Pearl's back. '*She's a bad influence!*' Liv was tucked in behind me, and Sage and Demi were up front as Marmal veered Pearl toward the Witch Lands.

'*This was always the plan,*' I told Luka. '*I kill Morgana and you kill Maz.*'

'*I know, but I thought I would be there just in case something went wrong,*' he said.

I looked at the other four badass women with me and chuckled. '*Luka, I'm in good hands. We totally got this. You should be as far from it as possible now that you are king.*'

He was silent. '*Tell me when it's done. Be safe. I want to marry you, not bury you.*'

'You will marry me,' I assured him. *'And, technically, it would be cremation since we turn to ash.'*

'Not funny,' he growled, and I grinned at my own joke.

Demi had a sour look on her face. I imagined she was arguing with Sawyer via their mate bond. It was bad timing with our big plans to bring down all of the breeder camps in just a few days, but I couldn't let this chance pass me by.

Pearl flew over Troll Village, the Fey Lands, and finally we came upon a landscape I didn't recognize: weeping willows, running creeks, and lush green rolling hills. It was beautiful, but it also had a charge to the air.

We started to descend the second we passed into the space and I frowned. "We're here?" I yelled over the wind, looking for Morgana's tent or cabin or wherever she was holed up, but all I saw were endless woods and farms.

"Slight problem." Marmal stroked Pearl's white scales. "Her invisibility shield went out the second we flew into the witches' space. It won't work here, so you will have to go the rest of the way on foot."

Demi nodded, and I did the same. I wasn't going to let a little bump in the road deter me from my one shot at taking out the psycho who'd filled my chest full of lead.

Once Pearl landed in a thick apple orchard, we slipped off of her and adjusted our weapons and packs.

"You stay with Pearl," Demi told Marmal. "I'll keep in touch through the pack link."

She tapped her head, stroking Pearl.

Marmal tipped her head in agreement and I looked at Liv.

"I know you're a badass, but this could get crazy, and I feel like we should have you help protect Marmal and Pearl?" Okay, I was kind of saying she couldn't hold her own in a vampire fight, which I knew wasn't true, but I just loved Liv so much and Morgana was crazy. She'd taken me out so quickly, even though I was a hunter.

Liv sighed and then nodded. "Be safe." She hugged me, and pulled out her sword, standing before Marmal and Pearl like she was their guardian.

With a grin, I followed Demi and Sage into the woods. Pearl and Liv and Marmal disappeared from view.

"You think she will still be there?" I spoke softly.

Demi nodded. "She's laying low in a small trader village. The reason we heard about her is because

Marmal recently visited some friends in Troll Village and trolls pay in gossip."

I frowned, unsure what that meant.

Demi read my confusion. "Some traders bragged about a strong female vampire hiding out with the witches and buying all of their pelts and paying them for blood feedings."

It *had* to be Morgana.

Demi looked down and consulted her map as we hiked through fields and orchards. We passed a homely looking witch who took one glance at us and just gave a startled wave as we popped out of her cornfield.

Demi waved back and the woman went back inside. "Sawyer has our helicopter on standby if we need an evacuation," Demi shared.

Nice. But I hoped we didn't.

Demi kept consulting a map and looking off, concentrating. I think she was mentally talking with her pack at the same time as navigating us. It must be a great burden to share your head with so many voices. I could barely handle Luka's.

It was about a half an hour walk through the countryside of the Witch Lands before Demi finally raised her closed fist and we stopped. We'd reached some kind of settlement. Up ahead, there was a

cobblestone road that led up a mountain, and lining the side were small brick houses. Some of them had solar panels. A mix of new and old.

This must be the trader village Morgana was laying low in.

Demi jogged behind a row of cottages while Sage started tossing off her clothes, getting naked.

Okay ... shifter modesty was not a thing.

It was daylight; my limbs felt heavy with sleep, which meant Morgana would feel the same thing.

After Sage shifted into her wolf form behind a small house, Demi pointed to a map and then to the next house over.

Morgana was last seen there.

With luck, she'd be sleeping and I could just yank her head off and be done.

"Did you really think you were going to sneak up on me?" Morgana's voice came from behind us. We all spun.

Shit.

So much for the element of surprise. She stood between two male vampires who were suited up in warrior gear, looking ready for battle. She grinned. "I could smell your little furry companions from a mile away."

Morgana's gaze ran over my body, her eyebrow raising.

"Did you think you'd killed me?" I shot back. Anger brewed just beneath the surface of my skin. She'd changed Luka against his will, planted the thought of killing his mom in his dad's head, and tried to kill me. If there was anyone who deserved the output of my unstable emotions, it was her.

Her two lackeys rushed forward then, and Sage and Demi ran out to greet them, clashing together.

Morgana, in a blur of motion, shot forward, and I rushed out to hit her head on with a battle cry.

'You okay?' Luka's voice came through our bond.

'Found Morgana. Not a good time to chat,' I responded as her fist connected with my collarbone and I felt something shatter. At the same time, I reached up and yanked a chunk of her hair out. Her shrill scream ripped through the air.

She looked at the hair in my closed fist in shock and I grinned. I wasn't above hair pulling. By the time I was done with her, she was going to beg for mercy.

My anger reached a boiling point. Something big, pulsing, and magical had built inside of me, and keeping it in was actually hurting. I threw my hands out and screamed in frustration. A shockwave of

power burst from my palms and slammed into Morgana, tossing her backward and snapping the trees in my immediate vicinity in half.

What the hell? I stared at my hands in shock. Did I ... do that?

"You're Ithaki!" Demi grumbled beside me as she fought her vampire. "Your fey power must have activated when you turned into a vamp."

I had ... *fey* powers?

Holy crap.

I was so stunned by the display of power I'd just shown that I didn't realize Morgana was already coming back at me. She had a dagger in her hand and was running so fast I could barely track her. Throwing myself backward, her knife hand barely missed, grazing past my arm, slicing into my flesh.

Being a vampire was crazy. She'd broken my collarbone a moment ago, and it had hurt, but already it felt like it was almost healed. Instead of worrying about the bleeding wound like I would if I were still human, I pulled out the stake from behind my back and burst forward. I stabbed at her like a maniac, punching six holes in her in rapid succession. All purposefully in non-kill zones. She gasped in shock as my weapon penetrated her skin.

"That was for Luka's family," I hissed.

Fear trickled across her face and she rushed backward and away from me. When she hit the tree line, she ran.

"She's fleeing!" Demi growled. Her legs were covered in dead vampire ash—so was Sage's muzzle. They'd already taken care of Morgana's henchmen.

Sage darted forward but Demi grasped her wolf by the middle and yanked her back. "This is Aspen's kill," Demi scolded.

Spurred on by that confidence, I took off into the tree line before Morgana could fully heal from the wounds I'd just given her.

I ran full-out, but Morgana was still a blur ahead of me.

She was fast, even in her injured state, and I was starting to wonder if I could catch up with her. I needed to throw another shockwave thingy. The other one I'd only done because I'd been full of rage.

'Quick, tell me something awful about what Morgana did to you,' I prodded Luka.

He didn't even ask why I wanted to know. *'If she hadn't poisoned my father's mind, my mother would still be here and able to attend our wedding. But she's not, and a small part of me will look out on that day and picture her in one of those seats.'*

Okay, this bitch was dead. So dead.

The rage ripped through me so fast and hot that I screamed as a slice of pain ran down my arms. I threw all the power I could at Morgana's back. It burst outward, knocking into everything in its path. Morgana soared forward onto her face as bushes and trees flattened. *Whoa.* Rushing faster than I ever had before, I reached her just as she was pushing herself up. I jumped on her back with my feet, pinning her down. A groan ripped from her lips.

Gripping the stake, I leaned down and whispered into her ear. "You'll never be queen, but thanks to you, I will be." With all the force I had, I slammed the tip of the stake into her back, right where her heart was, and she went limp. Her body started to decompose, drying out like a shell, turning to ash around my boots. By the time Demi and Sage ran up behind me, Morgana was gone.

They let out two whoops of excitement and I couldn't help but smile.

It's done, I told Luka.

Shock ripped through our bond. *'Morgana's dead?'*

'She is,' I told him.

'Are you hurt?'

'Nope. And I found out I have a cool new fey power.'

'Fey power!' he shrieked.

I chuckled. *'Tell you about it when I get home.'*

"Back in time for dinner, what did I say?" Demi beamed, and slung an arm around my shoulders. I couldn't help the high that came with knowing I'd actually killed a big baddie. My entire life at the society I was killing vampires left and right without really knowing which ones were true criminals. Morgana, on the other hand, she deserved it. The world was a better place without her in it.

We set out to find Pearl and Liv and Marmal with matching grins on our faces. When we finally reached them, they were sitting on Pearl and ready to go. Liv looked at me expectantly and I nodded, causing her to beam.

Morgana was down. Now we just needed to take care of Maz. She was the one I was really worried about. I knew Luka was strong—he was the king of the vampires—but if anything happened to him while he was carrying out a task for me, I would never forgive myself.

"Nervous?" Luka asked as I stared out the window of our bedroom. It was Friday morning and we had to catch our plane to LA in a few hours.

I turned to him, smiling. "Not really, just antsy to get it over with," I admitted.

He nodded and handed me his cell phone. "Milika texted. Everything is a go. The women and children are ready to flee, and I've got the maps we need."

I glanced at his phone and nodded. "Good."

"What's wrong?" Luka asked.

I frowned, reaching out to stroke his bicep. "I have a bad feeling. I can't shake it."

He tipped his head up to look into my eyes. "Just one more night, then we can put all of this behind us. Soon, fey using breeders to make vampire hunters will only be in history books, and we can have our happily ever after."

I chewed on my lip, unable to get this knot to unravel in my stomach. "I just hope it goes okay," I told him. "Our wedding is in a few weeks. I just want to make it down that aisle and then onto the rest of that night." I waggled my eyebrows.

He grinned like a fool. "I mean, if you're afraid of dying a virgin, we can fix that problem right now." He pulled me into a fireman's carry and tossed me on our bed. Peals of laughter erupted from my chest as he lowered himself over me, grinning.

I smiled. "I love you."

Leaning down, he kissed my nose. It was something he'd always done; it held such a tenderness that it made my throat constrict. "And I you, Aspen soon-to-be Drake. Don't die, because I really want to have sex with you."

I gave another burst of laughter and I smacked his chest. "And spend the rest of your immortal life with me."

He nodded. "Having sex."

My cheeks hurt from grinning, and I suddenly felt sad for anyone who had not experienced a love like this. A love so carefree and easy that laughing was second nature.

A knock came at the door and Luka pushed himself off of me, pulling me up with him as he went.

"Coming, Liv!" he yelled in annoyance.

Liv's muffled voice came from behind the door: "How did you know it was me?"

"It's always you." Luka rolled his eyes playfully.

Did he just mutter *cockblocker* under his breath?

He opened the door and I whistled at my bestie's getup. She was dressed in a short mini skirt and corset bodice. Her hair was pulled into two poufs, and she wore a smattering of glitter over her eyelids.

"Wow," Luka said, dumbfounded.

I grinned. "King Constantine is going to love you. You sure you're up for this?"

She tapped her ribcage. "Got some razor wire. If he gets out of control." She drew a finger across her throat.

Luka swallowed hard. "Remind me not to get on your bad side."

Ruby appeared down the hall and made her way toward us. She was on the phone, but hung up as she reached us. "Everything is in place. At about 8 p.m. tomorrow night, the dominos will fall."

This was it, whether we were ready or not.

"Let's roll." Luka grabbed our duffle bags and we headed out to the airport with our crew.

THE FLIGHT WAS EASY. We took a private plane, since there were fifteen of us in all. We didn't want to be too suspicious, so we traveled with ten vampires and five human "feeders" who were actually hunters from House of Thorns. The plan was that once the fights got underway, the "feeders" and five of our vampires, including me, would sneak away and lead the escape. Once we were clear of the city, Luka would make sure Liv and the others got out in the melee. Hopefully, the vampires would be focused on entertaining Luka so that I could slip away and lead the attack. The rest of House of Thorns was splitting up and going to society houses in all of the cities to take out the corrupted leaders there and liberate their people. Saying I was nervous that something was going to go wrong was an understatement.

By the time we got to the pho shop, it was late and the fey woman at the front waved us all through without having us pay. We were officially here as King Constantine's guests.

Luka checked us into the same hotel as last time, renting the entire top floor, and then we settled in for a time of rest. The Freedom Fight was at 2 a.m., so technically tomorrow but not really; it was just past 10 p.m. now. Getting used to all these different hours was hard for me, and I drifted off to sleep quickly.

"IT'S TIME." Luka shook me awake. I cracked an eye open and glanced at the clock, bleary eyed. 1 a.m.

Getting up, I brushed my teeth and put on make-up, quickly getting into my dress. Next, I stashed weapons under the poufy skirt and braided my glossy red hair over one shoulder.

"Problem." Luka stepped into the bathroom holding his phone.

My stomach dropped. "What is it?" I had a bad feeling this entire day and now he was going to drop some bomb on me, I could feel it.

Luka frowned. "Milika has been forced to enter the fight."

"No!" I shouted. "I thought it was something the people did freely of their own will?"

Luka sighed. "I guess this year King Constantine

has upped the ante and it's a mandatory assignment. If she doesn't fight, she will die."

That bastard. My heart plummeted into my stomach. "Well, we can't let that happen. She helped us, Luka."

"I know." He looked at me with agony in his gaze. "I'll figure something out."

"Tell her that. Tell her we've got her back." I pointed to his phone. I was nothing if not a woman of my word.

He tapped away on the keyboard, presumably texting her, and my stomach tied tighter into a ball of anxiety that felt like it would consume me. Something bad was going to happen, I just knew it.

Was a trap waiting for us, as we had laid one for the king? He was cunning and he had some outside friend in the know. Maybe he knew all along.

I just didn't know, but something was off and there was nothing I could do about it.

After everyone was ready, our group took a caravan of tuk-tuks. I was glad to see our werewolf driver Tink was back, and flagged him down in the line of cabbies to be our personal driver.

"Are you fighting tonight for freedom?" I asked him over the sound of the wind.

He just nodded quietly but said no more.

Hmm. Okay.

I mean, you couldn't exactly have a conversation while driving someone in an open pedal bike, but still … I'd given the man a multi-thousand dollar tip last time. The least he could do was be nice.

'He's acting cagey,' I observed to Luka.

'He's about to fight to the death, Aspen. It makes one cagey.'

Touché.

Ignoring it, I sat back and watched as we passed the market stalls and crowded stores, and then drove up the hill to the king's palace. There were thousands of white twinkling lights dotting the road up to his home, like you would use on Christmas. Not to mention a total traffic jam going into the gates. Our driver kept glancing back at me and then forward again.

Something was off.

"Did you ever get a hold of a fey blade? I could try to get one to you." I lowered my voice as we were stalled in the drop-off line.

He stiffened. "Why would you do that?" He glared back at me.

I frowned. "Werewolves are our equals where we're from," I told him.

Luka nodded. "My best friend is the alpha of the

Werewolf City pack in Idaho. He said that any of you who want to defect are welcome with him."

The dude bristled as if he was offended. "Alpha?"

Oh, that's right. Milika had said that alphas were against the rules here or something.

"Two alphas actually. Husband and wife. Mates. It's a long story." I chuckled.

The line started moving again, but he looked back at me with a worried glance. This time Luka noticed.

"You're acting strange, bro. You good?" Luka asked. Tink didn't respond as he pulled into the gates, the guard not even asking for invitations as there were so many people. He then careened the tuk-tuk off into a parking spot on the grass.

When he turned to finally face Luka, he wore a haunting expression. "I don't care about bloodsuckers, okay, but your woman did me a solid last time, so I'm going to tell you something." His voice was so soft that even with super hearing I had to lean forward.

Luka was as still as a statue and simply nodded.

The werewolf swallowed hard, looked at the front doors of the house, then back to Luka. "King Constantine wants your lady. Hasn't stopped talking about her since you left, says she makes him feel alive again. He intends to fight you once more. He will kill you this time and take her." He inclined his head to me.

Oh. Shit.

Luka didn't move an inch. "You're sure?" was all my fiancé asked.

The driver nodded. "I hook up with his assistant, Carmen, sometimes. She blabs the entire time."

That was the dark feeling I had carried all day. The king wanted to kill Luka to get to me?

Luka nodded. "Thank you. I won't forget this. I owe you. Come with us tonight when we leave."

The guy chuckled and pointed to his neck and the collar that rested there.

"Let me worry about that," Luka stated.

The guy shrugged. "I didn't say anything. You heard nothing from me."

We both nodded and he stepped out of the little makeshift vehicle and lit a cigarette.

"He asked if I had a friend. Liv?" I told Luka. Wondering how the king could be obsessed with me and ask for me to bring a friend.

"A cover," he growled. "So that I wouldn't question his mild flirting with you."

"But ... he'd have to be crazy to kill a fellow king," I whispered.

Luka looked at me, deadpan. Okay, he was slightly insane already.

"What do we do?" I asked.

Luka took my hand and kissed the top. "This changes nothing. Plan forges ahead."

"What? But he's going to try and kill you!" I whisper-screamed.

Luka nodded. "Yes. So ... I will have to kill him first."

Oh, God, help us. This rescue mission just went from hard to impossible.

"Ready?" Liv stepped up and shook her cleavage in my face.

"Yeah," I mumbled, and stepped out of the tuk-tuk as we assembled our crew. There was no time to fill everyone in on the new plan, they would just have to watch it all unfold live.

Awesome.

Luka linked arms with me and we led the group around the side gate, where guests were pouring in by the tens and twenties. We funneled through the entrance and I took in the scene before me.

Holy crap, it was five times as big as the event we were here for last time: more seats, bigger fighting ring, and a huge crowd packing the place from fence to fence. It seemed like the type of event you would have in an arena, but something told me the king liked to make this *his* thing, something he hosted at his house so he could be sure to take all the credit.

We moved through the crowd with our group. The ten vampires that Luka had brought split up with their "feeders" to visit the bar and other areas, while we went in search of the king to present Liv to him. His date. Whom he apparently didn't even care about.

Now I was regretting my skintight black ball gown with peekaboo cutouts.

"Mr. and Mrs. Drake!" Carmen's singsong voice trilled behind us.

We spun and gave her a bright smile. I tried not to envision her screwing Tink and talking about how the king wanted to kill my husband-to-be.

"King Constantine will be so happy to see you! Follow me." She expertly wove through the crowd and then we came upon an animal type pen. It had chicken wire and long wooden boards, but instead of animals behind the fence there were … people.

Slaves.

My hand clamped down so hard on Luka that he instinctively yanked away in pain.

'Sorry,' I muttered, trying not to look annoyed, because King Constantine was about to turn around.

The king spun and I pulled the corners of my mouth up into the biggest fake smile I could muster given the situation.

He beamed at us. "Oh, how lovely, my special guests have arrived!" He shook Luka's hand and then moved to me, letting his eyes roam slowly over my body, taking my hand and kissing it. "You look delightful, Aspen," he purred.

'I'm going to kill him slowly,' Luka growled.

"This is Liv!" I blurted out, spinning around to make room for my bestie to move forward. Liv looked nervous but also sexy as hell. The king's eyes glittered as he pulled her hand up and toward his lips. "Lovely Liv. We are well met."

She giggled and I ran my gaze over the trolls and werewolves in the giant pen. "Milika!" I blurted when I recognized the troll.

The king looked at me, perplexed. "You know someone in there?"

Shit.

"That's the one I told you about, darling." I yanked on Luka's right arm. "Can I please have her? She was such a help getting me ready for the dinner party last time."

Luka rolled with my acting. "Ahh, yes." He turned to the king, who had understanding in his eyes. "Can you sell me that troll? Aspen really needs a better lady's maid."

The king looked at me with a sparkle in his eye. "What Aspen wants, Aspen gets." He winked.

I'm going to cut his tongue out,' Luka said through our bond while still fake smiling.

"Let me pay you for her of course." Luka went to reach for money and the king waved him off.

"It's a wedding gift," he said, and signaled for Carmen to release Milika.

"Thank you so much!" I squealed, hoping Luka knew I was being fake. The way Luka's muscles pulled taut reminded me of a cheetah about to pounce on its prey.

After Carmen gathered Milika, the troll kept her eyes on the ground as she approached the king and I.

"You are to be Aspen's lady maid, understood?" the king told her, and she nodded rapidly, relief spreading across her features. Carmen used a key to uncuff the shackle around her neck, and I waved to the parking lot.

"Meet me in the parking lot at the end of the night. I have no use for you now," I said in the snottiest voice I could muster.

She met my gaze with a grateful look and then scrambled away. Liv hooked arms with the king then, distracting him from the fact that I'd all but freed her to go help the women escape when the time came. "I hear you like shots? I'm feeling rather parched myself."

The king grinned. "Then let's get a drink!"

Okay, Liv was doing this undercover escort thing way too easily.

'Carmen keeps the keys for collars,' I thought out loud to Luka through our bond.

'Yep. Good to know.'

Following the king and Liv to the bar, we had a seat and the werewolf bartender handed out drinks.

I held up a hand and declined. "I don't drink, but thank you."

The king raised an eyebrow, appraising me. "A virtuous woman. I adore that."

Luka growled but turned it into a cough. *'Okay, now he's asking to get punched.'*

I gave a nervous laugh and pointed to the stage, trying to bring the focus to my friend, who was his date. "Liv loves fighting. She does jujitsu."

"Is that right?" The king feigned interest but his eyes stayed on me.

Crap. The driver was right, he wanted me, which meant we'd just walked into the lion's den and we were way outnumbered if he sicced his men on Luka.

"I hope your friends from Idaho are enjoying themselves," the king told me, looking over at Ruby and one of Luka's vampires.

"I'm sure they are. They were very excited to come," I said politely.

Luka sipped his drink, shooting eye daggers at the king as he kept striking up conversation with me and ignoring Liv and him.

Liv seemed to catch on, because she gave Luka a *what the heck?* look.

A bell dinged before I could answer the king's question about how long we were staying.

Carmen came over the loudspeaker: "The Freedom Fights are about to begin!" And the crowd roared.

"Come, let's sit. I want you to meet a good friend of mine." The king stood and Liv eagerly hung on his arm. Luka reached out, grasped my hand, and the crowd parted as we made our way to the front of the mat where the high-backed chairs were. There were five chairs and it looked like one was already occupied, but I couldn't tell who was sitting in it. The figure was cloaked. Probably some powerful witch or fey.

As we reached the chairs, the king bent to the figure and pulled up their hand, kissing it. Must be a woman.

"I want you to meet my new friends from Idaho," the king told her.

She reached up and pulled back her hood to reveal short-cropped gray hair.

My breath stuck in my throat.

Maz.

She looked as shocked as I was to see her. Her eyes ran over Liv with absolute disdain, and then to Luka and I. "Hello, I'm Maz, King Constantine's business partner." She reached her hand out.

This had to be a trap? The king knew what we were doing and called her here. Right?

'*Go with it. King is clueless,*' Luka said.

I looked at the king to see that he was indeed looking at me and wondering why I wasn't shaking her hand.

"I'm Aspen." I shook her hand lightly and pulled back the second I could, remembering the freaking curse she'd put on me just the other morning.

"*King* Luka Drake," Luka stated, using his royal title for the first time in front of the king. Constantine bristled.

Could this night get any more shitty? I was just

waiting for Morgana to step out from the dead and say she regrew from dust or something.

The bell dinged again and the king asked us to sit, before stepping away to speak to Carmen. I reluctantly sat next to Maz and she leaned in with a grin on her face. "Did you really think I would let you take all I built? I have been watching you for weeks. I know what you're planning. It won't work."

Crap, crap, crap!

'Maz knows. She's here to stop us,' I relayed to Luka.

'I'm going to excuse myself and inform Ruby that there may be resistance at the brothel.'

Luka stood and I quickly switched seats as Liv took my spot. When the king sat back down, he was right next to me with a space between Liv and I for Luka. I was going to use his infatuation with me to the fullest extent possible.

"That lady is your business partner?" I asked quietly, indicating Maz, who was now speaking to Liv.

He nodded.

"Hmm, some business partner. I just heard her bragging on the phone that she cheats you out of your share?"

His face grew into a feral snarl. "What!?"

Maz and Liv looked over at me and I rested a

hand on his forearm, stroking it. "Now is probably not the time to deal with this," I whispered. "It's party time. But I would watch out for her."

He nodded to me and then glared at Maz.

Checkmate, bitch.

HOUSE OF ROSE

THE FREEDOM FIGHTS began and I watched in horror as werewolves and trolls beat each other bloody, all in an effort to get the shackles removed from their necks. It made me sick, but I clapped and cheered with the rest of the crowd. Luka sat on my right, while I stayed near the king and let him whisper things into my ear. He thought I knew nothing about battle and was teaching me what certain fight moves were called.

Idiot.

When the entire party was engrossed with the bloodshed, Luka made the call.

'Go now,' he mentally sent out to the entire vampire team we'd brought. They would inform the humans with them, like Ruby and her hunters.

I tensed, hating that I couldn't actually be there

when they got the women and children out, but trusting that Luka had picked the very best people for the job. If Liv or I left this area, it would trigger Maz or the king that something was up. We'd just have to rely on our team.

I tried not to bop my foot in nervousness as the mental silence stretched. Luka didn't talk about it much, but because he was king he had mental connections to his vampires, much like an alpha werewolf. He would be more in tune with what was going on than I would.

My attention drew to the next fighters getting ready. I recognized our werewolf driver, Tink. He was going up against a giant troll the size of a small car.

Crap. I didn't want him to die.

"Why don't you let them fight with their full powers? Seems like it would be more fun to watch." I winked at the king.

He absolutely melted under my gaze. "Is that what you would like to see?"

I nodded. What Aspen wants, Aspen gets, right?

The king stood, and beckoned Carmen with a flick of his wrist. He whispered something to her and she nodded. Walking over to our driver, she pulled out a key and unclipped his neck collar. His gaze burned into mine and I gave him a slight nod. Next, Carmen did the same to the troll.

The troll and wolf looked at each other in wonder. It brought tears to my eyes that it had been so long since they'd been free they didn't even know what to do.

"Let's spice things up, shall we?" Carmen called out into the microphone.

The crowd went insane, and then our driver started to shift. Fur bulked out on his arms, bones snapped; he hunched forward, panting, as the shift took over him. All the while the king watched my face for my reaction. I grinned delightfully, hoping I was as good of an actress as I felt.

The troll held out his hand and a scream of shock ripped from the crowd as a fey blade magnetically attached to his palm.

The king chuckled. "Let it be!" he cried as a fey rushed forward, seemingly to retrieve their blade.

It was obvious to me why the king didn't allow trolls and werewolves to be free. They were powerful and a threat to his crown. Why the fey bowed to him, I had no idea.

The bell dinged and the giant troll lunged at the wolf. I winced as the wolf leapt into the air and brought his jaws around the troll's arm. The crunch of bone rang throughout the space and everyone cheered. The troll used his free hand to swipe at the wolf's belly, but Tink released his arm and rolled to the side in time to avoid it.

'The team met some resistance with House of Rose, but they are in,' Luka told me.

My heart plummeted into my stomach. *Maz brought House of Rose here to fight against us?* My own people. The ones she had left that were still brainwashed, I guessed. It all made me sick. To be sitting a few feet away from her made my blood boil. Maz stood, and the king looked at her. "Leaving so soon?" he asked with slight annoyance in his tone.

Maz gave him a sugary smile. "Just using the ladies' room."

Yeah, right! She was going to foil our escape.

I stood as well. "I'll join you. I'd like to touch up my make-up," I told the king and Luka, clasping my purse, which had zero make-up in it. It's not like anyone would believe me if I said I had to pee since I didn't do that anymore.

The king gave me an approving look, as if he loved the idea that I cared enough about my appearance to want to freshen up midway through a night.

"Girls' trip to the bathroom!" Liv stood as well, and Maz looked so pissed her jaw ticked.

"Lovely," Maz growled, and we all left.

Luka's voice in my head was an ominous warning: *'Be careful. Remember you can't hurt her but she can hurt you.'*

Liv was strong, a great hunter, but up against a Munai …it would spell her death. I didn't need to hurt Maz, we just needed to incapacitate her for a bit so our team could get the women out.

I grabbed Liv by the upper arm and pulled her back and away from Maz.

"Go get the collar Carmen just pulled off the wolf. I have an idea," I muttered as softly as I could.

Liv's eyebrows hit her hairline, but she nodded.

I picked up the pace, following Maz into the house as she took out her cell phone. Reaching out with blinding speed, I snatched her phone and snapped it in half. A few partygoers looked in my direction.

Maz simply stilled, a small flicker of her illusion fading as the anger took hold of her. I could see her grotesque demon-like appearance just beneath her skin.

"I'm sorry. Did you need that?" I asked her.

"You're up to something. You don't want me to check in with my team," she growled, and stepped deeper into the hallway.

She was going to flee.

I stalked forward as she moved backward. "What team? The one who came to Vampire City asking for help recovering from your brainwashing and lies?"

A snarl ripped from her throat and her illusion fully dropped for a moment. "Mind your own business, Aspen. Leave Los Angeles and the other cities to me," she snarled again.

I laughed. "Not. On. Your. Life. *Bitch.*"

She lunged for me and I threw myself forward, wrapping my arms around her wrists before she could throw a spell. The second my hands clamped around her forearms, an intense pressure came around mine.

My eyes widened and Maz grinned.

"Oh yes, darling," she purred. "You won't be harming a hair on this head."

I had a flashback then of when I was six years old and I'd been playing at the park with the other orphans. I'd tripped and skinned my knee and cried. Maz had been the one to rush over and comfort me.

"Why do you do it? We loved you," I whimpered, unable to come to grips with the fact that this motherly figure had turned out to be such a psycho.

She looked at me with disgust. "Vampires think

they are superior, but anything that needs blood to survive is an abomination in the eyes of the Lord."

I frowned. I couldn't really fault her for the blood comment. I agreed it wasn't natural. "And a Munai?" I asked. "A dark witch who throws black shadows and inky nets? If anyone is a demon, it's *you*!" I spat.

She yanked her wrists from my hold and charged forward. I was helpless to stop her, lest I do harm to myself. All I could do was brace myself for the hit. Right when Maz was inches from me, Liv jumped out of nowhere and snapped the collar around Maz's throat with a click.

Maz's entire body seized as she seemingly tried to do magic and was thwarted.

"Go! I got this," Liv called to me. "The king just challenged Luka to a *friendly* fight."

No. He was going to try to kill my man while I was in the bathroom touching up my make-up? How gentlemanly.

Bolting out the hallway and through the kitchen, I burst outside to the roaring crowd. Tink was injured but alive and Carmen was looking around frantically, no doubt for his collar.

Where was—?

The king and Luka were pounding into each other on the mats.

'Finish him!' I called to Luka through our bond.

'I have to let him try to kill me first so it's in self-defense. Otherwise his people will charge forward and finish me off.'

Shit. This was a nightmare. I was living in a nightmare.

I could only pray that Ruby and the others were getting the women and children out, and that Austin, Chicago and the other cities were cleaning house, because right now I had bigger problems to worry about.

I perched on the edge of my seat and made a promise that if it looked like the king was getting too close to killing Luka, I would insert myself into the fight and take him out.

Luka sprang up to his feet and picked the king up, holding him above his head as all of the blood vessels in his face bulged. Then he tossed him in the air so high that when he fell, the ground shook.

Whoa.

The crowd burst into applause and the king flicked his gaze in my direction. I raised one eyebrow, hoping to convey my confusion at the situation. He erupted up from where he stood and grabbed Luka in a chokehold.

My fiancé went very still then, and the king

yanked his head, probably intending to rip it off. A scream ripped from my throat, but Luka must have sensed that was the king's intention, because he jumped upward, working with the king's motion, and crashed his head into the king's face. With a growl, the king released his hold on Luka's neck and staggered backward.

The crowd fell silent and I stood. "He's trying to kill him! We were invited as guests!" I shouted, hoping to make people see what was going on, because I knew Luka was about to kill the mad king. Or at least I hoped.

King Constantine roared in laughter and then looked at me. "I admit you are far too pretty of a prize to let go."

Luka snarled at that, charging forward, but the king zipped to the side and grabbed a silver stake that just happened to by lying near Carmen.

How convenient.

Bastard.

All fighting rules had gone out the window. Whatever gentlemanly arrangement this was had soured, and the crowd noticed. They remained silent, eyes glued to the center mats as the men duked it out.

Well, if the king wasn't going to play by the rules, then I wasn't either.

You mess with my man, you mess with me.

Emotionally unstable Aspen was feeling stabby. Reaching down beneath me, I gripped the chair leg in my hand and yanked upward, snapping it off. It broke away in a perfect pointy tip.

Standing up, I surged onto the mat to stab the king in the back. One of the king's men leapt forward to attack and intercept me. There was a blur of gray fur and then Tink leapt through the air in wolf form and attacked the vampire's neck.

Most of the crowd gasped, but some cheered, and I sidestepped the fight with the werewolf and focused on the king. Luka had fallen to the ground and the king had his fist raised, stake in hand and ready to come down on Luka's heart.

I raised my arm just as Carmen yelled for the king to turn around. I brought my fist down with such force into the king's back that the stake pierced his heart and he was thrown forward, onto the mat just beside Luka.

The crowd took a collective gasp and Luka sat up, looking at me in surprise.

'I had that,' he tried to assure me.

'Mmm hmm,' I replied.

I glanced at the king, whose skin was starting to shrink and turn to ash. But before it did, I caught a good look at his face. He was … smiling.

"You set me … free," he whispered and then turned to ash.

What. The. Hell?

'He was crazy,' Luka told me.

Tink had killed the vampire who'd tried to attack me, and now came to stand at my side, as if waiting for direction from me.

"She killed the king!" someone yelled, and the crowd started to press forward.

I gulped and Luka stood, stepping in front of me and Tink.

"My name is King Luka Drake!" he bellowed, and the crowd fell silent. "I rule the vampires in the magical enclave in Idaho. King Constantine was mad. We were invited tonight as his guests, but he just wanted to steal my wife. I'm sorry we've caused trouble here, but this was self-defense."

The crowd didn't say a word, they didn't move. They seemed in shock.

One old fey stepped forward, her pointy ears sticking out of the top of her hair. "He's been king for over five hundred years. What do we do without him?"

Five hundred years!

Luka pointed to the cage of trolls and were-wolves. "For starters, you can cut off their collars. All supernaturals should be treated equally. Then you can vote and have a quorum led by one representative from each race. Live in harmony."

Without waiting for a response, Tink shifted to his naked human form and stepped forward, ripping the fey blade out of Carmen's hand. He then started to cut the collars off of all of the slaves in the holding area.

A murmur rose up behind us as the people realized that this would change the entire way their world worked.

By the time they had even given the idea much thought, the trolls and werewolves were all free, and now stood behind us, almost challenging the crowd to disagree.

An older fey woman nodded. "Everyone go home. We will meet here again tomorrow and vote on the next steps."

Tink stepped forward. Thankfully he'd found some pants. "And the werewolves and trolls will be a part of this vote, right?" His tone was laced with threat.

The fey woman's nostrils flared but she nodded.

"Moving forward, I think it's best everyone is involved in the decisions we make for Night City. *Equally.*"

She looked at Luka and I.

Luka grasped my hand. "We are happy to serve as … consultants … as you build your new world. Give you information on how things work peacefully in our world."

The fey woman nodded. "We will be in touch, then."

Luka pulled my hand. *'Let's go before this unravels. They are still in shock, but it will wear off soon.'*

I looked back at our driver. He was grinning ear to ear.

He was going to be okay … they all were. Even Milika. It was the best case scenario. Somehow, in all this mess, we'd gotten a good outcome.

"But she killed the king!" someone shouted as we made our way for the exit.

'Maz is trying to stop Ruby and the breeders from escaping,' Luka told me.

Shit. I'd almost forgotten about Maz! That meant…

"Liv!" I ran through the tightly-packed crowd with Luka hot on my heels. Bursting into the kitchen, I turned the corner and yelped at the sight of Liv crumpled into a ball, unconscious. I bent and put my fingers to her neck and then realized I could still hear her heartbeat. She moaned and I sighed in relief.

"I got her. Let's go." Luka swooped his hands under her legs and the rest of our crew filtered into the house.

"Let's get out of here," one of Luka's guards said, and we nodded.

We raced to the line of tuk-tuks. Luka's guards jumped behind the wheels and took off, not even waiting for drivers. I leapt into the back of one and Luka slipped beside me with Liv still in his arms.

"You can put me down, Romeo," Liv grumbled.

Luka rolled his eyes. "You're welcome."

Liv slid off his lap and sat next to me. I pulled her in for a side hug. "You okay?" I asked as the tuk-tuk barreled toward our planned escape exit.

Liv grabbed the side of her head and looked up at me. "She cut the collar off like it was made of butter."

"I'm going to take care of her," Luka told Liv with a growl.

The king was dead. We had nearly freed the people. The pit in my stomach should be gone, but it wasn't.

THE EXIT PLAN that we had in place was to ferry the women and children out of the southernmost exit of Night City. According to our maps, it was a pizza shop on this side that came out in a seedy little clothing store in the fashion district in Downtown LA. It was the least guarded and the least well known. We barreled toward that area, passing super-naturals left and right. Seeing the wolves and trolls still chained broke my heart, but I knew it would take time for the revolution to spread in this city.

As we turned the corner and made our way to the pizza shop exit, I gasped.

There was a standoff. The House of Rose hunters and Maz were standing in front of the pizza shop, weapons drawn, while the five House of Thorns hunters we'd brought, mixed with a handful of

Luka's vampires, tried to pass them with the dozens of women and children they had freed.

Anger shot through me at the sight of it, and I leapt out of the moving vehicle, barreling toward the hunters. I zoomed down the street and skidded to a stop before House of Rose.

"How dare you!" I shouted at the hunters I once trusted. "I showed you evidence. How *dare* you side with her." Bridgett, Nathan, Kyla … all of my supposed friends were standing with Maz, their weapons drawn.

Bridgett's face faltered. "You're kidnapping these poor women and children."

I chuckled. "Is that what she told you? These children are future hunters, and we're freeing them."

One of the women held a newborn baby, only days old. "That's right," she called out. "So let us pass!" She looked paranoidly over her shoulder as if she expected the king to come after her any moment.

Bridgett frowned, lowering her sword.

"Don't listen to these lies!" Maz screamed, raising her blade. "Aspen has been fornicating with a vampire and now she's one of them!"

It was as if she'd desecrated my honor or something, because Luka went ballistic.

Charging forward, he knocked right into her like a bowling ball, throwing her back onto the concrete. The House of Rose hunters spun on Luka, weapons raised. And that's when Maz lost the hold she'd had over her illusion.

Gasps rang out across the street as for the first time they saw Maz for what she really was. A black inky net flew from her mouth with a scream and wrapped around Luka.

"Help him!" I shouted to his guards. I was unable to fight Maz, but they could.

"Go on!" I told Ruby and the others. "Get them out of here."

If Maz heard that we'd killed the king and upset the balance here, I wouldn't put it past her to take over this place and make it more evil than it already was. Luka needed to end her. Now.

House of Thorns pressed forward with the women and children, and the House of Rose hunters just stared dumbfounded at the woman who'd raised us—the woman who'd always had short salt and pepper hair and a kind smile was now flinging living black shadow bombs and snarling like a demon.

I stepped forward and grasped Bridgett by the arm and she stiffened, looking at me in surprise.

"Go," I told her. "Help Ruby and the others get

the women and children out. You don't have to see this."

The pain, confusion, and trauma I saw pass behind her eyes made me slightly sick. Knowing that your entire life was a lie was almost too much to bear, but if Liv and I could get through it, then I knew she could too.

With a nod, she pulled the other House of Rose hunters into the pizza shop, leaving just Luka and his men to fight Maz.

"Problem," Liv said from behind me, and I turned. A group of local vampire and fey stepped out of the shadows. "She killed the king!" one of them shouted, and then they all rushed forward.

Crap.

Luka and Maz were locked in battle, so Liv and I had no choice but to fight off this horde together and give him time.

She looked at me, pulling the razor wire from her bra and grinning maniacally. "Happy hunting."

I chuckled. Just like old times.

"I'll take the fey," I shouted, indicating the three pointy-eared folks advancing with arms outstretched.

She nodded and jogged toward the two vampires. I felt for the weird magic that got ignited when I was angry. It felt dark and mysterious, and quite frankly it scared me a little. It was there, just below the surface. I grabbed hold of it and then pushed. A shockwave of invisible hot gasses or whatever shot from my hands and plowed into the three fey. They flew back, and the glass from the surrounding buildings blew outward, shattering.

Oops. A bit of overkill.

"A little help!" Liv barked, and I spun just in time to see her take a vampire's head. But another was barreling down on her. Meanwhile, Luka arced through the air and landed in a heap. His men were fighting a second horde of locals that had come from another alley.

It was complete chaos.

'You okay?' I asked Luka as I attacked the vamp on Liv's back.

'Yep.' He launched upward and dealt a blow to the side of Maz's head.

Once Liv and I had taken care of the vamps, we shifted our attention to the main fight. Maz was attacking Luka with everything she had, but he was a beast, tearing through her defenses like they were nothing. It looked like he had wrested her fey blade from her and was lashing out with it. When they clashed together this time, I saw the glint of steel in

Luka's hand. I froze, unmoving, as I watched him seemingly in slow motion as he rammed the blade into her neck.

Maz opened her mouth, letting out a roar, throwing black sparks from her hands in a hopeless attempt at survival. The sparks shot out like bullets and then died completely as Luka took her head clean off.

My chest ached as I watched my beloved mentor of so many years meet her end.

"Aspen…?" Liv's distressed voice called to me.

I turned to face my best friend, expecting that she sounded so upset over seeing Maz die. But a strangled cry ripped from my lips.

Liv was holding her stomach. Black veins were growing outward across her skin. She'd been … infected? Cursed? I didn't know, but whatever it was looked bad, and was moving fast.

"Luka!" I screamed, rushing to catch Liv as she collapsed into my arms.

Her lips turned black and I stared in shock as whatever Maz had thrown at her took hold.

"Shit." Luka grabbed her from me and shook her, as if that mere act would stop the progression or whatever was happening.

"What is it!?" I sobbed, watching as the blackness took over the whites of her eyes.

Luka swallowed hard. "I think … it's a curse of some sort. We have to hurry."

I didn't need to hear that twice. Whatever he was planning in order to save Liv, I was down.

We rushed through the noisy pizza shop, and then into a hallway that would lead to Los Angeles. There was a witch crumpled up against the wall; the door that led to a store full of fabric was open. One lone man wearing headphones sat behind a sewing machine in the corner and paid us no attention. Luka handed Liv to me the second we stepped into the shop and pulled out his phone.

"I need Astra," he said, and then, "Good."

"What's going on?" I started to sob because Liv's head lolled against mine as she lost consciousness. She didn't look like my Liv anymore. She was starting to look … *like a Munai*. Her eyes rolled back in her head, completely dark. Her hair was turning dark too. What the frick?

"I had Demi and Sawyer standing by in case we needed help. Their … friend … is special. She's a healer. It's a lot to explain but you have to trust me. I've seen her do this before."

All I could do was nod. Luka took Liv from me as

if he were pulling a ragdoll from my arms; her neck flopped to the side.

No.

"Hurry!" We bolted from the store, unaware of our surroundings or where Ruby or any of the others were. I no longer had a beating heart and yet it felt like it was going to jump out of my chest. Luka was holding my entire world, my sister, my best friend. We'd raised each other; she was family, she was everything. An uncontrollable sob ripped from my chest as we crossed the road and Luka looked over at me. "Have faith."

My weeping stopped immediately and chills broke out on my arms. He was right, I couldn't unravel now. Liv was a good soul. I needed to have faith she wasn't going to die on me. Not now. Not so young and *not* at the hands of Maz.

We reached the other side of the street and I looked around desperately for the familiar face of Demi.

"Where...?" I stopped when the door to the van right beside us swung open and then Demi was there.

"Get in here." She indicated her head into the van as Sawyer stepped out to make room.

"I'll go help the women and children get on the bus," Sawyer told Luka.

I grabbed Liv from Luka's arms and told him to follow Sawyer.

"You sure?" he asked with a worried glance.

"Yes. Go," I snapped, and then leapt into the open door, wasting no time. It slid shut behind me with a snap and I looked around.

The van was completely gutted in the back except for a mattress and some open potato chip bags. A young girl with short-cropped, mousy brown hair sat cross-legged on the mattress, and looked up at me with big blue eyes.

"Aspen, this is Astra. Our Paladin priestess." Demi moved back to give me room to fully look at the girl, and for her to see me as well.

Her gaze fell on to Liv in my arms and she smiled, full of joy and innocence. "Oh, she has so much light," Astra said.

Tears streamed down my face as I fell to my knees and laid Liv before her.

"Can you save her?" I begged. "Please."

She looked at Liv's black lips, the black veins that crawled up her neck, and then reached out and pulled one of her eyelids up.

Black.

I sobbed.

"Soul transfer. Whoever did this is trying to stay alive by using Liv's body," Astra said.

Soul. Transfer.

What. The. Frick. Was. That?

Maz was still alive? Inside of Liv? Is that what she was saying?

"Can you help her? I'll do anything!" I begged again.

Astra held out her hands. "Pray with me?"

My best friend was infected with Maz's black soul and she wanted me to pray? I took in a deep breath, even though I didn't even need oxygen, and nodded.

God was the only one that could save her now. I wasn't sure if she was even still breathing.

"Father..." Astra looked up at the roof of the van, smiling. "There is so much light left in her. If you would have her be saved, then please use me as an instrument of your healing." She bowed her head and I just stared at her in awe. She was all of sixteen or seventeen, and so sure of herself and her faith. It was incredible.

A gasp tore from my throat when blue shimmery magic started to fall from the ceiling of the van and onto Astra. She let go of my hands and raised hers up to catch the magic. I stumbled backward as she then laid her hands on Liv and the blue mist coated my best friend like a second skin.

Her body jolted, her shoulder slamming up and then down on the bed. More mist fell, covering Liv's entire form so that I could no longer make out her dark hair or eyeshadow. She was like a blue being. Her body jerked again and I looked at Demi.

The alpha reached into her thigh holster and pulled out what I recognized as a fey blade.

Interesting, what was she going to do with th—?

Liv opened her mouth, screamed, and a black inky blob ripped from her throat. Demi rushed forward with the blade and hacked into it, as it had suspended in midair, shredding it to pieces. It disintegrated before my very eyes.

Was that Maz's soul? Because I wasn't sure I could handle the fact that it had just possessed Liv!

The blue healing magic fully absorbed into Liv's skin and then she gasped, eyes snapping open. I threw myself over her, sobbing and hugging her like a crazy woman. Her eyes were normal, no more black veins. She was healed. I sat up and wiped my own eyes, looking at Astra in awe. She was so small and unassuming. You wouldn't guess how truly blessed and powerful she was by merely looking at her.

"Thank you," I croaked, pulling her into a hug as well. Her arms wrapped around me.

"What just happened?" Liv asked dreamily.

We all burst into laughter and I pulled back and peered down at Liv, so glad to see her looking like her normal self.

"Maz is dead. Her soul jumped into you. But it's all going to be fine now." I grabbed her shoulder and she shrank away from me.

"Who's Maz? Who are you?"

My stomach dropped. And then Liv burst into laughter.

"Are you kidding me? You thought that was funny!" I reached out and punched her shoulder, hard.

"Not cool," Demi agreed.

Liv sat up. "Sorry, it was too serious a moment. I needed some lightness."

She turned to Astra and tilted her head to the side. "Thank you."

Astra grinned. "Welcome."

"Yeah, like seriously thank you. Is there anything we can do? Like pay you or something?"

Astra shook her head vigorously. "No, no."

I frowned. "Well, will I see you again? Maybe I can buy you lunch next time I'm in Werewolf City?" I would sit there and not eat food like a vampire weirdo.

Astra and Demi shared a look, both of them grinning.

"What?" I looked at them both. They were obviously hiding something from me.

"It's a secret," Demi told me, "but Luka got Astra to officiate your wedding."

My heart pinched and butterflies took flight in my stomach. I'd told him I wanted a holy person to marry us and he'd chosen Astra?

I looked at Astra with tears in my eyes. "That's perfect."

She reached out and squeezed my hand. "Can't wait."

There was a knock on the van door and Demi reached out and opened it. Luka was standing there, grinning.

"All good?" He looked at Liv.

She nodded.

"Why are you smiling?" I asked him.

He consulted his phone, which was buzzing with text after text. "We did it. All of the women and children across all of the cities have been freed. The corrupted leaders of the societies are gone too."

The relief that crashed through me was so sudden that a strangled cry ripped from my lips. Liv's arms wrapped around me, and we both held on to each other.

Liv pulled back from me finally and looked up at me. "What now?"

"Now we rebuild it better than before," I told her.

There was nothing wrong with wanting to fight evil and protect the innocent, but we needed to rebuild the society in a way that was transparent. In a way that Maz never could. We needed the truth, no matter how painful it was.

THE PHONE RANG and I ran across the office with super vampire speed to pick it up. "Supernatural Protectors Guild, this is Aspen."

Ruby and Liv gave me a thumbs-up from where they sat at their desks and I put our first phone call on speaker. "Hi, I'm in need of some protection. I've got a really psycho fey ex-boyfriend who's stalking me."

I nodded. "Okay, why don't you set up a time to come down to our office and we can map out a plan to keep you safe."

"That would be great," she said.

"I'll forward you to our appointment line," I told her, and pushed the button to pass her off to Liv.

Liv's phone rang and she picked it up with a grin. Holly, Anthony, Valerie, and all the House of Thorns hunters were here too. They stood by excitedly, suited up for work.

I gave a silent whoop in the air and the main line rang again. "Supernatural Protectors Guild, this is Aspen."

"Woman, you better not be late to our wedding," Luka growled.

I grinned. "We're leaving in an hour! I'll be there on time." My hair was already done and the dress was in the break room. When Ruby, Liv, and I got the idea to open our own supernatural hunter guild here in Vampire City, Luka gave us the barn that the House of Thorns' hunters had been staying in. It only took a few weeks to convert it to an office, and we'd accidently made opening day the same day as my wedding.

"Love you." Luka's dreamy voice came over the line.

"Love you too." I hung up and the phone rang again.

When I answered, it was an older werewolf woman who needed security for a big party she was having on her farm. I patched the call through to Ruby and smiled. It wasn't vampire hunting, we weren't taking down the big bads in the human world, but it was a start. All of the houses sort of crumbled after they learned the truth that the vampires and supernaturals in their area weren't all bad, and most of them hadn't committed any crimes.

I knew they needed time, like I had. They would find their way to something that made sense, like the SPG did for us.

We were part hired security and part private detectives. It soothed the ache that was caused by all of Maz's lies. And it was safe enough for me to let my lil' half-sister Maple get involved. When she walked in with my mom, she was wearing an SPG t-shirt with logo. A walkie-talkie was hooked onto her belt, next to a can of pepper spray. She took the new job *very* seriously.

She stepped up to me and saluted. "Reporting for duty."

I grinned. "Big day today. You sure you would rather do this than be my bridesmaid?"

She rolled her eyes. "Of course! Lead security for the biggest wedding in Vampire City. It's an honor," she told me.

I grinned. I didn't expect anything to happen at the wedding, and if it did we had Luka's royal guard, but my little sis wanted to feel important, and if this helped do that, then so be it.

"Just don't mace anyone unless they really deserve it," I told her.

She pulled her walkie out and pressed a button. "Copy that." She winked and the corresponding walkie on my mom's hip squawked.

We all laughed, and then my mom walked over to me and pulled a stray hair from where it was stuck to my forehead. "You look beautiful. I never thought I would see the day that you—" Her voice gave out and I pulled her in for a hug.

"You're the best thing that came out of all this," I told her as we held each other tightly.

"Okay, now we really need to get you in your dress!" Liv called out behind us, and my mom and I broke away wiping our eyes. Ruby's team stepped in to take over the phones as we all moved to the employee break room to get ready for my wedding.

Once my make-up was done, I was just slipping into my dress when there was a knock on the little office break room door.

"Come in if you're not Luka!" Liv yelled.

I grinned. "It's Sage and Demi. I can smell them."

The door burst open and Sage rushed forward, arms above her head. "It's wedding time, bitches!"

We all laughed, and Demi stepped in behind her

carrying a medium sized box. "Got you a prezzie," she said, handing it to me.

"Aww. You didn't have to do that." I cracked the lid, expecting to see a custom t-shirt or something, but when my eyes fell on the jeweled tiara I had tried on and liked in the vault room, I gasped.

"Demi ... I can't." I stroked the jewels with my fingers.

She smiled. "You totally can! I cleared it with Sawyer and his mom. It's yours, as a symbol of our friendship with Vampire City."

Liv reached over my shoulder and pulled it out. "Okay, don't expect this nice of a gift from me," she joked, causing us all to chuckle.

I tilted my chin down and she placed the tiara on my head. When I raised my head to look at my three closest friends, they all had tears in their eyes.

"You look like a queen."

Queen of the vampires. Who would have thought?

"Come on, let's get you to the chapel!" Demi whooped.

I chuckled. "Vampire City doesn't have a chapel."

Sage, Liv, and Demi all shared a look. "Right. Totally right," Demi agreed.

I tossed her a glare. "What are you hiding?"

Demi chewed her lip. "Nothing! Come on."

With that, they pulled me up and out to my wedding.

WE WALKED the short distance to the castle garden, which was where Luka and I had decided to get married. It was pretty and carried better memories than the main hall, where I'd watched him kill so many people. When we reached the main entrance that would lead to the garden, Liv took a right turn, away from it, in the direction *behind* the castle.

"This isn't the way," I told Liv, but Sage and Demi just pushed me in the direction Liv was leading.

"Hey. I don't like surprises on my wedding day!" I pouted.

They just shushed me, and as we wound around the castle gates, a faint music started to prickle my ear. I grinned.

'What did you do?' I asked Luka through our bond.

I could almost feel him smiling. *Just wanted to make my new wife comfortable in her new home and give her the wedding of her dreams.'*

A grin tugged at my lips. I had no idea what to expect, but I knew it would be wonderful, just like he had been since the day I met him. The odds had been stacked against us and yet we prevailed. We grew stronger, we fell in love.

When we turned the corner so that we were directly behind the castle, a gasp flew from my lips. Tears immediately filled my eyes. I had to rapidly blink to clear my vision.

He'd built me a church. The man whom I'd once called a demon because my false religious upbringing had poisoned me had built me a church.

"Don't cry!" Demi hissed, patting my cheeks.

"Mascara running!" Sage started to dab under my eyes and I laughed.

I didn't know where I stood with God now that I survived off of blood and had killed a lot of people without cause—but I did know that God was forgiving, just like Luka had been to me.

So when I walked closer to the church and threw the doors open, I had zero hesitation for wanting to marry the man of my dreams. I trusted him with my heart and soul and everything in between.

The music changed the second I entered, and every eye looked up at me. The chapel was small, and yet that made it even more amazing. It only seated about forty people, and it was packed to the gills, with others standing outside. The light coming through the stained glass was breathtaking. Pictures of angels were set into the colored glass in broken bits.

A peaceful feeling settled over me.

I'd never been more ready to spend my life with someone than I was right now.

When my gaze went to the end of the aisle, it locked on to Luka.

'I'll never forget this,' I told him, looking around the church in wonder. *'This is the best day of my life.'*

The grin that swept across his face made my knees go weak. Luka Drake was totally out of my league, yet somehow he wanted to marry me. He didn't care that I'd hated vampires when we first met, or that I was a virgin, or anything else. He accepted me for me.

When I reached the end, I saw my mom and Maple sitting in the front row and gave them a wave. Maple tapped her mace and winked at me, causing me to chuckle.

Luka stepped forward and pulled me into his arms. "You look stunning, My Queen."

Queen. Holy crap, I kept forgetting I was going to be queen!

Saying Luka looked stunning would be an understatement. Seeing him now in his black tuxedo made warmth rush between my legs.

Sawyer, Bennet, Walsh, and Talon stood behind him.

Five Crew.

We'd been through hell together, each of us separately in our own way, but we'd all made it out alive. Well, mostly, since I was technically undead.

Astra's singsong voice pulled me back to the present: "Aspen Rose and Luka Drake … it is my honor to bless this union."

We faced her, holding hands as she read a beautiful poem about love and declared us man and wife. By the time "kiss the bride" was said, I wasn't ready for this picturesque moment to be over. I just wanted to take it all in.

We made our way to the reception, which was being hosted in a giant white silk tent that had been erected on the lawn. There were hundreds of people inside of varying supernatural races. When I recognized Milika and Tink, I looked at Luka in shock.

He winked. "They wanted to pay their respects."

I broke away from him and rushed to give Milika a hug. Tink was looking as strong as ever, and free of his collar, although he still carried some of the scars.

"I'm so glad you both came!" I told them.

Milika smiled shyly, and Tink dipped his head to me, a cigarette tucked behind his ear. "We wouldn't miss it."

"How are things? I mean ... do you need to come and live here? We'd love to have you," I told them.

Milika grinned, sharing a conspiratorial look with Tink.

"I'm the alpha now, with a seat on the quorum," Tink said. "Trolls have a representative too."

I couldn't help the grin that splashed across my face. He'd always seemed like alpha material to me.

"I've been relieved of my debt. I work for Tink now," Milika told me.

Tink slung an arm around her, looking down at her like a cherished little sister. "That's right. And no one messes with my people." He winked at her and she blushed.

Okay, maybe not a sister.

"Just wanted to officially thank you in person," Tink added, "Enjoy your night. I'm going to teach this one how to dance."

Milika squealed and he pulled her onto the dance floor, leaving me with a light feeling in my chest. Knowing what they'd been through, for them to still have such zest for life, it really touched me. I peered around at House of Rose, House of Thorns, werewolves, vampires, trolls—people had come from all over to celebrate Luka and I, and I felt so blessed.

"Boo," Liv called behind me and I spun, laughing. Luka stood next to her, watching me with an adoring gaze.

"I smelled you coming from a mile away," I told her. "You'll never be able to scare me again."

She rolled her eyes. "Whatever. I got you guys a joint gift. Not a million-dollar tiara, but still cool."

She handed Luka and I a piece of paper and I raised one eyebrow in anticipation. Was it skydiving lessons, because I would totally do that now that I knew I couldn't die. Luka flipped open the page and I scanned it over his shoulder, unsure what I was seeing. It looked like Liv had some medical tests done or something.

She grabbed her belly. "My baby maker is fully functional, and the werewolf doc says I should be able to carry a baby for you … ya know, if and when you want. I know the council is bugging you for an heir, and you've always wanted to be a mom but—"

"Liv!" My throat tightened with emotion at her priceless gift. I crashed into her with a hug.

"Are you … sure you wouldn't mind?" Luka's throat cracked; he seemed overwhelmed with the offer.

Liv knew how badly I wanted to be a mom, and the vampire council wasn't exactly waiting long for Luka to produce an heir. With my eggs frozen and Luka's sperm…

"I don't know what to say." I squeezed her harder.

"Too hard," she yelped, and I relaxed my hold as we both burst out laughing.

When I pulled back, she was grinning. "My present was better than the tiara, huh?"

I chuckled. "A hundred times better."

Vasquez stepped up beside Liv and held out his hand. "Dance with me?"

She looked at me and I shrugged.

"She already promised me a dance." Talon, Luka's troll best friend, stepped out of nowhere and extended his hand. Liv looked surprised for a second, like she'd done no such thing, but then grinned and took Talon's outstretched fingers.

Vasquez frowned and then walked off, sulking. I might actually feel bad for him if he hadn't cheated on her.

"Dance?" Luka pulled me into his arms as the band played a romantic slow tune. I took his hand and let him twirl me around the open space until the food was served.

Our guests that actually ate food started in on

their dinner, while Luka and I sat at a table and listened to speeches by Liv and Sawyer. They were horribly embarrassing and hilarious, everything a best man and maid of honor speech should be.

As the night pressed on and we danced and visited with everyone, I leaned in and whispered in Luka's ear.

"I'm ready for bed." My words were innocent, but my hand on his inner thigh wasn't.

"Me too." Luka stood so abruptly the table moved six inches. I burst out into laughter and he scooped me up into his arms.

"My bride is tired! Thank you all for coming!" Luka shouted, and everyone raised their glasses in a cheer. Then, with vampire speed, he rushed us out of the reception and through the castle grounds, until seconds later we were in our room.

I couldn't stop grinning. "Someone's eager."

"Woman, you have no idea," he growled, and started to unzip my dress while he peppered my neck with kisses.

I was slightly nervous, but not enough to stop me from unbuttoning his pants and letting them fall to the floor. My dress dropped around me, and then I was just standing there in a white thong and no bra.

"Dammit, you're perfect," Luka growled, as he took me in from head to toe.

"And you're too clothed." I eyed his tuxedo jacket and button-down shirt. Stepping out and over my giant dress, I slowly unbuttoned his shirt. Leaning forward, I planted a kiss to his lips and sucked his bottom lip into my mouth. When the moan ripped from his throat, pure need opened up inside of me.

"I'm ready," I huffed against his mouth as I ripped the last remaining buttons off and he was naked before me.

"Are you sure?" He pulled back and looked at me with glowing yellow eyes.

I nodded, stepping out of my panties.

His gaze raked over my nakedness. He gave me a predatorial look. "Lie down."

Delicious anticipation washed over me as I backed up and lay on the bed. Luka slowly crawled on top of me and kissed his way up to my mouth. I felt his hardness against my stomach, my breath coming out in ragged gasps as I prepared myself to give the only gift I had for him.

I never would have guessed that the man I'd been saving myself for all my life would have been a vampire. Life was funny that way.

"DON'T LIFT A FINGER!" I snapped at Demi, Sage, and Liv. I moved to grab the boxes in the entryway to Sage and Walsh's new house as Luka, Walsh, and Sawyer came in behind me.

The three pregnant women looked at me with annoyance.

"We're pregnant. Not handicapped!" Demi snapped, holding her six-month pregnant belly.

Sage rolled her eyes. "Yeah, and Demi and I are werewolves, we can handle lifting a box." Sage was five months along. She and Walsh got pregnant right after her wedding.

"I'm fine not lifting a finger. I'm going to milk this with everything I got!" Liv exclaimed, and we all chuckled. Liv was nine months pregnant and ready to pop any day now. She was carrying a beautiful, healthy little girl for Luka and I. Modern science was amazing, and the fact that two vampires were about to have a pretty much human baby was kind of insane.

She would be seven percent Ithaki, and Luka and I agreed we wanted her to stay human and just be the way she was born unless she chose otherwise. Luka was working on dissolving the laws that required a king to have a vampire heir. We hoped one day that our daughter could rule the vampires as a human, or they could find someone else in the Drake lineage, but we wouldn't force a change on her like it had been forced on us.

"You're right," Sage exclaimed to Liv. "Let's go in the kitchen. I have chocolate peanut butter ice cream."

"Yum," Demi and Liv said at the same time, following Sage into the kitchen. I stayed close behind their three waddling butts and tried not to feel sorry for myself that I couldn't carry my own child. I was going to focus on the positive. The fact that I was a vampire and could even *have* biological children was amazing.

Twenty minutes later, the girls were halfway through their ice cream when Liv winced.

"What's wrong?" I zoomed to her side, hand on her belly.

She looked up at me. "It's fine. It's been happening all day. I'm just gassy or something."

Sage and Demi shared a look. Both spoons clanked into their bowls. "Gassy or contractions?"

Uncertainty flickered over Liv's face. "I mean, they don't really hurt. It just feels hard."

"Those are contractions!" Demi sputtered.

I whipped out my phone. "I'm texting the midwife." Because Liv was Ithaki, we had a supernatural midwife right here in Werewolf City. Coincidently, she was the one who would be delivering Sage's and Demi's babies too.

"Oh!" Liv leaned forward and grimaced. "Now they hurt."

Shit.

'Luka, Liv's in labor.' I had barely sent the mental message to him and then he was there in the kitchen holding a box marked "garage stuff" and staring at Liv with wide eyes.

My phone buzzed and I looked down. "Midwife is on her way to the hospital. She'll meet us there."

Demi and Sage both squealed. "You're having a baby!"

Excitement thrummed through me. I looked at Liv. She was almost green with anxiety.

"Remember, I get an epidural or we never speak again," Liv warned as she stood.

I laughed. "Whatever you want." I grasped her by the arms as she hunched over in pain.

Luka drove like a cautious maniac to the Curt Hudson Memorial Hospital. By the time we pulled in, the midwife was waiting in the lobby. After getting Liv checked in and hooked up to an epidural, Luka and I camped out by her bedside and whispered words of encouragement as she listed every single cuss word imaginable between grunts and screams. Talon showed up halfway through and offered words of encouragement to his girlfriend. Apparently, the epidural didn't fully work on Ithaki, and Liv's fey side was rejecting the medication.

Oops.

"I hate you," she growled in my face.

"I love you. Thank you for this gift," I told her.

"It's the only kid you'll ever have," she shot back, red-faced and in pain.

"You're amazing," I coached her.

"Shut up," she growled, and then gave a final push. When our daughter popped into the midwife's hands with a full head of dark hair and crying, I burst into tears.

Liv collapsed back on the pillow. Talon held a washcloth to her forehead and she looked up at the ceiling, panting. "I did it."

Luka reached over and pulled the sweaty pieces of hair away from her forehead, leaning in to kiss it. "You did."

It was such a tender moment, one I would cherish forever. The next thing I knew, the midwife was handing me my daughter.

She was so beautiful. I wanted to treasure every moment with her, but I also wanted Liv to see what she'd done for us, who she kept safe these past nine months in her belly. Bending down, I placed the baby on her chest. "This is your Auntie Liv."

Liv stilled, looking down at her. Tears streamed down the side of her face as she stroked our baby's forehead. "Hey, kiddo." Then Liv looked up at me. "What are you naming her?"

Luka and I hadn't decided. He'd left it up to me. "I was hoping to keep the tree thing going. I was thinking Juniper, June for short."

I looked at Luka and he grinned. "Little June Bug it is."

Liv handed her to Luka and I stepped over beside him, looking down on her.

"Drake. Party of three," he said, and I grinned.

Our little family had grown, and our hearts had too.

The End

Here is what is coming up next from me! *Shadow Angel* is co-written by myself and Julie Hall. It's an action-packed Angel and Demon Urban Fantasy, set in New York City. Live on Amazon January 21st preorder here.

Ingram Content Group UK Ltd.
Milton Keynes UK
UKHW020434210323
418888UK00018BA/411/J